THE HAPPY HOUSEKEEPER'S GUIDE TO DISASTER

BLYTHE BAKER

Copyright © 2024 by Blythe Baker

All rights reserved.

No part of this book may be reproduced in any form or by any electronic or mechanical means, including information storage and retrieval systems, without written permission from the author, except for the use of brief quotations in a book review.

Something strange is going on next door. Suspicious that an elderly neighbor may be in danger, Barbara and her friend Vicky investigate mysterious activities down the street.

Barbara also has worries further from home, as a certain attractive but crooked restaurant owner has discovered the part she played in his downfall. Can Barbara uncover the truth next door without being blind to a more shadowy danger across town?

1

"This is so nice. I'm so glad that you thought of this."

I smiled across the backyard table at Vicky as she dabbed some red paint onto a trio of holly berries.

"I agree!" exclaimed Rose Miller. She beamed at me, some of her fine, blonde hair swirling in front of her pretty, slim face. "I can't remember the last time I had this much fun."

"I'm glad you all could be here," I said, brushing some excess green paint from in between my fingers. How was it that paint managed to find its way into the most bizarre places?

"Thanks for letting us bring the kids, too," said Harriette Webb, glancing out into the yard where a group of four young kids all played together, ranging from ages three to seven. "I don't think my mother could handle the three of them." She wore her long, dark hair up in a scarf today, in the same sort of style that I liked to wear. She had more style than most of the women in town did, and it was one of the reasons we had gotten along so well when we first met.

"And my husband's working, so I wouldn't have been able to come otherwise," added Rose, rinsing her paintbrush in the jar of water I'd set out on the middle of the table.

"What good is a treehouse like that if it can't be enjoyed?" I asked with a grin. "Besides, the twins were happy to share it since they're at school."

The wind picked up, swirling the few leaves that Craig hadn't had the chance to rake up into little cyclones to the delight of the kids playing in the backyard. Squeals of delight filled the air, a happy chorus backdropping our morning.

"Ah..." Harriette breathed happily, taking a seat in one of the cushioned, wicker chairs on the back porch, a fresh cup of steaming tea in hand. "We should make this an annual tradition."

"Agreed!" Vicky said, taking a step back to look at our work.

It had been my idea to have a garden tea party, but somehow it had morphed into something different all together. I still ended up serving good, hot tea, but what I'd hoped to be an elaborate dinner party with lanterns hanging from the trees in the backyard had morphed into a quiet morning get together with some of the new friends I'd made during my time in Cobbsville.

Vicky had introduced me to Rose at one of the school bake sales I'd gone to back in October, and we'd all three hit it off immediately. Harriette was a more recent introduction, but I appreciated not only her complimenting of my dress by designer name, but also her quick wit and bright personality.

It hadn't surprised me to find out that all these ladies knew one another, and so it seemed to make perfect sense when I invited them all over to spend the morning together.

"This was a great suggestion, Harriette, by the way," I said, sliding one of the mostly dry holly leaves off to the side of the brown paper spread across the table to make room for new ones. "Craig will be happy to see some decorating done this year."

"He hasn't done much since his wife died years ago," Vicky said with a frown, selecting one of the few decorations that were still untouched. "Hardly any lights. His trees have been more than a little sad, too."

"I'm not going to let that happen this year," I said, picking up my paintbrush to continue my own ornament. "I want the boys to have the best Christmas they've had in a few years. I think they deserve it."

Harriette smiled. "You're not even their mother, but you're definitely loving them like you are."

My face flushed. "I didn't really know that you could care for someone so fiercely," I said.

"Aww, Barbara…" Vicky said with smile. "That's so sweet."

I shook my head. "I thought they hated me when I first got here. I worried they'd think I was trying to be like their mom. But over time, we've started getting along, and I think they like having someone else in the house."

"I've heard Craig say that you brought a life back into the house that was sorely lacking," Rose said. "He told my husband that he didn't know how much they needed a woman's touch around, but it's made all the difference in their day to day lives."

"I didn't know he'd said that," I said.

Harriette smiled. "Don't think he wanted to hide

it or anything. He's just never been very good about telling anyone what's on his mind."

"That's absolutely true," I said.

"So..." Vicky said with a chuckle, glancing at me over the top of her own teacup. It was a good decision to serve something hot today, since a consistent chill had settled into the northern Georgia mountains in the middle of December. "Tell us who's got your eye these days."

I blushed harder. "Oh, I – There isn't anyone," I said.

Harriette laughed while Rose shot a knowing look over at Vicky.

"There most certainly is," Harriette said.

"No, there isn't," I said with a laugh. "Really. Not without trying, though."

Vicky, eyes twinkling, looked around at the other two. "She's been out with the mayor *and* the vice mayor."

"We don't need to talk about that," I said.

"I take it that you went out with the vice mayor before he was arrested?" Harriette asked.

"Harriette, don't tease her," Rose said. "What about the mayor? Why didn't that work out?"

"Too pretentious," I said with a wave of my paintbrush. "I had enough of those kinds of men back in Liberty City."

Rose studied me. "You didn't leave someone back there, did you?"

I looked away. "No. I definitely did not."

"Uh oh," Harriette said. "Heartbreak?"

"In too many ways," I said.

"Oh, don't worry too much, honey," Vicky said with a grin. "I'm sure we know someone eligible in this town of ours. Why, I was just asking Robert if his friend Michael was still available. He's a doctor in Kurkland."

"A doctor? That might be a good match if she wants to be wealthy and all, but what about having someone who is actually home once in a while?" Harriette asked. "My cousin married a doctor, and she and the kids don't see him but three or four times a week. It's not been a good adjustment for them."

"That's okay, everyone," I said. "Seriously. I think it might be best for me to take a step back from romance for a little bit."

"I'm not surprised that you turned some heads," Rose said, picking up the teapot I'd brought out and set on one of the small, round folding tables that Craig liked to use for the boys when he didn't want to eat inside. "You're pretty, for one, but also brand new. New can be exciting sometimes, and since most people in this town know each other, it's little wonder that you and your big city personality would be attractive."

Big city personality? Why do I not like the sound of that?

"Mama!" called the youngest boy. "Look at my leaf!"

"It's great, sweetie!" Rose called. "But – oh, Jonathon, please don't eat it – "

Harriette chuckled as Rose raced off the back porch and through the grass toward her son.

"So?" she asked, looking back over at me with a glint in those dark green eyes of hers. "What was it like going out with Milton Adams?"

My face colored. "Well, the date wasn't so bad... except he accused my brother of taking bribes. So there was that."

Harriette's smile disappeared at once.

"It's okay, it's all been worked out," I said. "Everything's fine."

"Why did he think your brother was taking bribes?" she asked.

I glanced at Vicky. She'd started to paint tiny initials in the corner of each of our holly leaves so we would know which ones belonged to each of us. I'd already shared all this with her. "Because it was actually his vice mayor who was doing that," I said. "He and my brother would meet regularly to discuss what was going on in the city, and Stewart would use what he'd learn to go out and make some money. From what I understand, the people conducting these less than savory deals were all too willing to pay him off to ensure that their goings-on did not reach the mayor's ears."

"Is Milton Adams really that stupid?" Harriette asked.

"Not stupid, no," I said. "He definitely knew something bad was going on, but he just thought it was the sheriff. My brother was the one who found out all these things were happening, and he wanted the mayor to be made aware. He and Roger Elwood only have so much time to look into the tips that people had brought to the police station."

"That seems like a pretty bad idea to start a relationship on a false accusation like that," Harriette said.

"That was my thought," I said. "Milton even tried to get me to spy on Craig. I refused." I sighed. "He did try to give me this gorgeous diamond bracelet as payment. I would have liked to have kept that. Call it payment for even listening to his idea."

"I bet it was a shock to your brother to learn all that," Vicky said.

"I think it was. He had gotten to know Stewart Wilson pretty well, so learning he'd been feeding him these means by which he got involved with the bad side of town instead of helping take it down..."

"Not so good," Harriette said.

"No, definitely not," I said.

"But to catch the eye of the mayor?" she grinned. "I bet you managed to meet some movie stars or singers back in the city."

I laughed. "If I ever did, I never knew it. I was just an ordinary woman out there, same as here."

"Except your brother's the sheriff," Harriette said with a laugh.

"And your father owns the best grocery I have ever been to," I said. "That's the best thing about this little town. Everyone is related to someone who is making it work so well."

"That's a very kind way to look at it," Vicky said. "And you are so right. What a wonderful way to enjoy and appreciate our home."

"I don't know, it gets boring around here once in a while," Harriette said.

"You should be thankful it isn't more like Liberty City around here," I said. "It isn't nearly as glamorous as everyone thinks it is."

"Do you ever miss it?" Vicky asked.

I considered for a second, then shook my head. "Honestly, I don't. I thought I did at first, but the longer I'm away from it, the more I forget what I liked."

"Wasn't it nice to have everything you wanted so close by?" Harriette asked. "My husband and I went to visit once for a long weekend. We got to enjoy the seaside *and* the downtown life with all the shows and restaurants in the same day."

"Sure, but that's not something you get to do every day," I said. "In fact, you hardly ever get to do that when you have to work and have other responsibilities. It's not vacation every day."

"I guess that makes sense," Harriette said.

Rose wandered back up onto the porch, tucking her bare hands beneath the arms of her thick, knit sweater. She glanced warily over her shoulder at her son. "You would think that if something didn't taste good he wouldn't keep eating it, but that's not how he thinks." She looked at me. "And not to jump into a conversation I wasn't a part of, but I've heard that when you live in a place, you sort of take it for granted. You start looking everywhere else and think that everywhere else is more exciting just because it's different."

Harriette grinned. "It's not that I don't like this little place, it's just that I guess everything feels a bit mundane sometimes. Maybe that just makes it feel boring."

"I don't really know if you could call it all that boring," I added. "There's been some rather unorthodox things that have gone on in the past few months."

"What, you mean the murders?" Vicky asked. "You only know about that because of your association with your brother. I don't think you'd think anything was going on if it weren't for him pulling back the curtain for you."

"Maybe," I said. "That could be it. I might not otherwise have found out about all this, would I?"

"You would have read about it in the paper, much like the rest of us," Rose said. "I'm sure we all still would have talked about it."

"True. Murders aren't really something that we see a lot of around here, are they?" Harriette asked.

"No, definitely not," Vicky said.

"Let's not talk about all that," Rose said, her arms wrapping more tightly around herself as she shivered against the cold. "It'll ruin the mood. This is supposed to be a little Christmas get together, not an episode of a detective TV show."

Harriette laughed.

I went inside and grabbed some more sandwiches for the kids, all of whom came rushing up onto the porch to grab them before hurrying back to the treehouse.

I took a seat next to Rose, and the four of us watched the little ones play together.

"I see Mr. Thompson hasn't decorated this year," Vicky said a few minutes later, breaking the silence. She pointed across our yard to the fence that separated our yard from our next door neighbor's.

"Craig said the same thing," I said, following her gesture. "He isn't really all that surprised. Mr. Thompson is getting on in years, and last year he nearly fell off a ladder trying to string some bulb lights up along the roofline."

"Oh, dear..." Rose said. "That's not good."

"Maybe Craig could help him," Harriette said. "I'm sure he's thought about offering, maybe just hasn't had the time."

Vicky shook her head, crossing one leg over the other. "Mr. Thompson's son Gerald should have helped him. I can't imagine why he hasn't, other than he's just lazy."

"That's a low opinion of him," Harriette said. "How do you know he's lazy?"

"My husband has talked to him a few times," Vicky said. "He told me that the man clearly lacks any sort of direction or gumption. When Robert asked him what he did for a living, he said that he'd been let go from his job at the post office and that was why he'd moved in with his father."

"But that doesn't necessarily mean he's lazy," Rose said. "Maybe he's got himself a new job that keeps him busy, and that's why he hasn't been able to help his father with any of the Christmas decorations."

Vicky shook her head. "No. As far as I am aware, Gerald doesn't work at all. He just sits at home all day."

"I didn't know anyone else was living with Mr. Thompson," I said. "I've never seen anyone else."

Vicky held a hand out toward me. "See? Proving my point."

"Maybe he works the night shift somewhere and has to sleep all day," Rose said. "I'm just trying to give the poor man the benefit of the doubt."

"He hardly deserves it," Vicky went on. "The way

he treated my husband. He's just like his father, always so rude and unpleasant."

"Come on, he can't be that bad," Rose said.

I nodded. "Old Mr. Thompson isn't all that nice. One afternoon just a few weeks ago, the boys were playing with a soccer ball here in the backyard. Toby managed to kick it over the fence and went to get it. Mr. Thompson hollered at him for being so careless, telling him that if he'd broken a window he would have made Toby pay for it himself."

"Wow," Harriette said, eyes widening. "Toby's just a kid."

"That's nothing compared to what he did to my oldest," Vicky said, now becoming annoyed. "Last summer, he went door to door with a fund raiser for the football team. While he was out, his dad went with him, and they went to Mr. Thompson's door together. Mr. Thompson practically chased the two of them off his front porch with his cane, saying that he'd rather give money to an alligator."

"That seems a little harsh," I said.

"He told my husband that he better keep the money they collected for himself, since we would need it to pay for all the brain damage our son would receive playing football," Vicky said, shaking her head. "Every time I would see him rocking on that rocking chair on his porch, I would wave to him and call hello. He'd just sneer at me, or ignore me all together. 'What's so good about today?' he'd say. 'We're just one day closer to death.'"

"You're kidding," Harriette said.

Vicky sighed. "Now it seems like his son is just like him."

"Sounds like it would be a pretty miserable house to live in," Rose said, eyeing the house warily over the top of the fence.

"You know...I can't actually remember the last time that I saw Mr. Thompson," I said. "It has to have been at least two weeks."

Vicky's brow furrowed. "I think I just saw him come out to get the mail the other day..." Then she shook her head. "No, that was before Thanksgiving."

"When I saw him, he looked like he was heading down to the street for a walk, but his son came out after him and escorted him back to the house," I said. "So I guess I *have* seen the son, I just didn't know he was living there full time. That was...oh, gosh, the Halloween decorations were still up?"

"Maybe his son doesn't trust him out by himself," Rose said. "I know a family that had to intervene for an older gentleman – grandfather, I believe – because he was starting to lose his memory and would wander out into the street looking for his dinner coat."

"Mr. Thompson is pretty sharp," I said. "The few times I've spoken with him, it's been clear that he's still got his mental clarity…nasty as it was."

Vicky wasn't looking at us. Instead her gaze had focused on the Thompson house.

"What's the matter?" I asked. I recognized that contemplative look. We might not have known each other for more than a few months, but she had shared what might have been her most private stories and secrets, and because of it, I knew her better than most people ever would.

"I don't know…" she said. "You said his son brought him back inside?"

"Yes," I said. "Why?"

She pursed her lips, her expression worried. "I don't know," she said again. "I thought I saw Mr. Thompson at the window one morning, and then Gerald came and moved him away, pulling the curtains closed behind him."

An uncomfortable feeling tickled my spine. "Do you think his son is trying to hide something from him?" I asked.

"I don't know, I – " Vicky started.

"Shh!" I said, my heart leaping into my throat. "Here he comes."

The back door of the house next door swung open, and Mr. Thompson's middle-aged son strode out onto the narrow back porch. He carried a black trash bag tightly in his fist, his eyes downcast.

"Just act naturally," Rose said, immediately reaching for one of the holly leaves and a paintbrush.

No one knew what to say or do. The awkward silence pressed into my eardrums, making my teeth itch. I didn't even want to open my mouth to talk. Anything that came to mind felt out of place.

I looked over just as Gerald hoisted the trash bag into one of the pair of trash cans along the side of the house. He wasn't paying attention to his trash bag, though; his eyes were on us.

My mouth went dry, but I raised a hand. "Afternoon, Mr. Thompson."

He just stared at me, and then the three women sitting beside me.

"Hello, Gerald," Vicky said with a nervous smile. "How's your father doing?"

Still the man said nothing, He stared at us like a deer spotted in an open field.

"Okay..." Harriette said underneath her breath,

getting to her feet. "I'm just going to go check on the kids."

"Me, too," Rose said, quickly catching up to Harriette, the two walking side by side down the stairs.

After a long pause, Gerald turned somewhat mechanically and headed back toward the porch. He disappeared through the door a few moments later.

"That was odd," I said. "That's the first time I've ever seen him doing chores. I swear that I've barely caught a glimpse of him since I moved into town."

"I believe you, as scarce as he is," Vicky said. "He…looked a little guilty, don't you think?"

"Guilty?" I asked. "Awkward, maybe, but do you think he looked guilty?"

"I don't know," Vicky said. "Why didn't he answer us? He could have at least said hello."

I frowned. "He did look a little like we'd caught him off guard," I said. "It's not as if it's everyday that there is a yard full of people next door. But is that not what he's usually like? Awkward?"

"I hardly know him," Vicky said. "Only met him once."

"I wonder if the elder Mr. Thompson's fallen ill or something," I said. "It might explain why he's been scarce, and why his son is doing things I normally see the father do. Though old Mr. Thompson typically takes his trash out after dinner."

"That would explain a lot," she said, then sighed. "He is getting on in years. It might not be all that difficult to imagine."

"I wish he would have answered us, instead of just staring like that," I said. "We could have offered our help or something. I wonder if his father likes chicken soup."

Vicky brightened. "Oh, that's a great idea!" she said. "We could get some meals together for them and bring them over. Even if he's just a little under the weather, it always helps to have one less thing to worry about, especially something like food."

"Then maybe Gerald will talk to us," I said.

"It's a plan," Vicky said. "Why don't we both make a meal and a dessert? I've never known anyone to turn down one of my pecan pies."

I smirked at her. "And yet you were the one who was just saying you thought Gerald was acting strangely."

"He was," she said. "If I'm honest, I'd like to know why he was acting that way."

I glanced over the fence at their house, my brow furrowing. "Yes, I'd like to know, too. Better than speculating over here."

Her smile slipped a little. "We should be careful. Sometimes families like to keep their secrets, and for good reason."

"I can understand that," I said. "We all do different things for different reasons, don't we? Just because we don't think they're a particularly nice family doesn't mean that they aren't able to function more normally when it's just the two of them."

"Right," said Vicky, her tone suggesting that she was trying to convince herself of it just as much as I was.

I swallowed hard, looking away.

I did not like the idea of something *else* being wrong in Cobbsville. We'd been through so much. Even Vicky and I together had been through more than enough.

I spotted Harriette and Rose in the yard, playing with the kids; they'd started a game of tag now that their sandwiches were finished, and the two mothers were doing a good job of giving the kids lots of space and time between catches. Kisses and hugs quickly followed.

"You know…" I said, slowly, deliberately. "I hate to even suggest this…but if there is something going on over there…something between Mr. Thompson and his son…"

Vicky's eyes met mine, and I saw a glimmer of understanding.

"They're our neighbors," I said. "Don't we owe it to them, and ourselves – our kids – to figure out if there's something wrong?"

I could see the hesitation in her gaze, but the resolve in her clenched jaw impressed me. Vicky might have seemed like an ordinary housewife with a typical family, a happy husband and children...but she was not easily frightened. She'd been through too much, seen too much, suffered secret troubles in her past...and this normal life was her reward. It was all she ever wanted. She'd told me multiple times.

A dark cloud settled over the yard, bathing the end of Pine Street in shadow.

A chill raced down my spine.

"Yes," Vicky said, holding her head high, her gaze set. "We have to know."

2

"How was the party?"

The wind blew outside the back door, which I kicked closed upon my return.

"Great...until the storm blew in," I said, sweeping a few dripping strands of my red hair from my eyes.

Craig reached out to take hold of the tray I had brought in with me, the teacups sloshing with rainwater. He smiled sympathetically as I grabbed for one of the dish towels and wrung my hair out. "I'm glad to hear it," he said. "The boys were sad to have missed it, but I think it's good that you had the party for you and your friends. The twins probably would have been too rough for those little ones."

"They sure enjoyed the treehouse," I said,

peering out the rain-streaked window. I could hardly make out the boy's retreat up in the old, southern oak in the yard.

"And the ladies?" Craig asked, dumping the water into the sink.

"Everyone had a fun time," I said. "I think we all made half a dozen holly leaves. I just hope they aren't completely ruined by the rain."

"They'll be all right," he said, eyeing the painted, wooden decorations on the kitchen table that the women and I had brought in first to dry. "I think you got them in here in time."

I sighed, shaking my head. "Apart from that, everyone had a nice time, I think."

"Well, it gave me an idea, something I shared with Roger," Craig said. "I think we're going to have a Christmas party at the station."

"Really?" I asked, shrugging off the coat I'd thrown on to finish cleaning up the rest of the things I'd abandoned outside when it started to pour. "Is that not something you usually do?"

"We haven't for the last few years," Craig said. "I always have Roger over for Christmas Eve dinner, but since our group at the station is so small, it never made sense to have a whole party."

"So...what changed this year?" I asked, running

my fingers through my hair, trying to get some of the tangles out.

"We wanted to throw a party that could serve the community," he said. "Give us a chance to see what's been happening but also to give people around town the chance to get to know us a little better. Makes sense, doesn't it?"

"It definitely does," I said.

"I was wondering if you'd want to help me come up with a theme for it and maybe help decorate," he said.

I laughed. "Oh, is that why you're bringing it up?"

"I thought you'd want to know ahead of time instead of me springing it on you," he said with a small smirk, retrieving his coffee from the counter behind him. "I know better than to do that to a woman."

"Well, I thank you kindly for that," I said. I sank down into one of the seats at the table, looking around. "Thanks for helping me clean up, too."

"Don't mention it," he said, and he slid a plate in front of me with a pair of bologna sandwiches.

I looked up at him. "You even made me lunch."

He smiled. "Thought you might like it after having your party rained out a little early."

He joined me at the table, and after a little bit of maneuvering of the decorations, we were able to begin our rather humble meal of sandwiches and sweet tea.

"Vicky noticed something interesting today," I said.

"Oh, yeah?" Craig asked, licking some mustard from his fingertips. "She's a pretty sharp one. What'd she see?"

"Mr. Thompson doesn't have any Christmas decorations up," I said. "No lights, no wreath, no tree in the window."

Craig chewed methodically for a moment, looking at me blankly. "...So?"

"She said that was kind of strange," I said.

"He's getting on in years," Craig said, echoing Vicky's words from earlier. "I can't imagine it's all that easy for him to get up on a ladder and take care of that stuff."

"Yes, but...Vicky was saying that she's worried that she hasn't seen him lately. That made me realize that I haven't seen him, either. I usually catch him walking down to the mailbox or out onto the driveway for his newspaper."

Craig shrugged. "He's probably staying inside

since it's getting colder. He never liked this time of year, always wishing he was further south."

"But that son of his…" I said. "Is he all right? He seems a little odd, too."

"He certainly is odd," Craig said. "Hardly ever talks to me when I see him. Likes his privacy, like his dad."

"He came out to drop off some trash in his garbage can outside today during our party, and he looked like he was surprised to see other human beings going about their day in the yard next door."

Craig's brow furrowed. "What are you getting at?"

"Vicky and I are wondering if maybe the elder Mr. Thompson has just taken ill and he and his son don't want anyone to know," I said.

Craig's head tilted. "Why would you assume he's sick?"

"Because his son never wants him to be outside," I said. "Always brings him back in. He even closed the curtains on his father, according to Vicky."

"That's not good reason to think he's sick," Craig said.

"Oh, yeah? Then where's he been the past few weeks?" I asked.

"Well, if he's sick, then it's really none of our business – "

"What if it's terminal?" I asked, and Craig went quiet. "What if it's fatal?"

Craig studied me, his eyes sweeping over my face. "I really think the two of you are overreacting about this," he said. "Mr. Thompson is a crotchety old man whose son likes his privacy. Nothing more."

"But Craig – "

"Barb, you're jumping at shadows," Craig said. "I know that you haven't been here that long, but Mr. Thompson is reclusive when it suits him. Now that his son is there to take care of him, he probably can be even more so. I've seen his son take some of the responsibility around the house, even more so recently. They must have made an agreement for him to move back in when Mr. Thompson's health started to decline or something."

"Which is my point!" I said. "Gerald was acting a bit odd when he was out back today – "

"And that's none of our business," Craig said. "Barbara, we can't chase every problem in Cobbsville. Even if there is something going on, that's their family and we can't get involved."

"Even if something's wrong?" I asked.

"Unless it's catastrophically wrong, then no. We

have to let people make their decisions. If they end up being mistakes, they'll have to live with them. But it isn't our job to try and control every aspect of every life around us. That'd be wrong."

I looked down at my empty plate. Some dirt had collected beneath my fingernails, likely from my frantic grabbing of everything on the porch in the rain. I picked at it, cleaning it out. "You're right…" I said. "I'm sorry."

"This is something you'll get used to," he said, smiling at me. "It was something I had to learn. I can't save everyone from everything, even painful things. My job is to make sure that everyone is as safe as they can be, so they can be free to live their lives as they please…within rational reason, of course. No pyromaniacs here, please."

I smiled, albeit reluctantly.

"…And I guess now would be as good a time as any to let you know that I finally had a chance to stop by Ricky Booker's place," Craig said.

I stiffened, my eyes snapping open wide. "And?"

"I didn't find anything."

I stared at him in disbelief "I'm sorry…we're talking about the same Ricky Booker, aren't we? The one who owns *Mer* downtown?"

He nodded. "The same. I went down there and he welcomed me with open arms."

I sighed, sagging right there at the table. "He knew you were coming."

"Well, between your interaction with him and what I told Stewart Wilson before we learned everything we did about him, I shouldn't have been surprised. I hoped that by going down early in the afternoon before he'd even opened, I might be able to catch him off guard..." He pursed his lips. "It was like someone called ahead of me to let him know I was coming."

"And you didn't find anything?" I asked, exasperated.

He shook his head. "That basement that you described? Spotless. Empty. There were even some convincing stacks of boards and buckets of paint, tarps thrown over a lot of it. Booker stood there with a sneaky smile on his face, lying through his perfect teeth as he told me about all the renovations he had planned. I knew he was lying, and he knew that I knew, and he kept doing it all the same."

He sighed, shaking his head. "I had nothing, apart from your word for what you saw. And unfortunately, that's not proof enough."

I sank back against the back of the chair, looking squarely at him. "You're kidding. After all that – "

"He's a weasel," Craig said with a shrug. "Too slick to be taken down so easily. I knew that going in."

"But you tried anyway?" I asked.

"I hoped I could catch him when he wasn't expecting me," Craig said.

I groaned, dragging my hands down my cheeks. "What do you suppose tipped him off?"

"I'm guessing Stewart Wilson," Craig said. "I'm guessing Ricky visited Stewart in prison, and he warned him."

"They're that good of friends, huh?" I asked.

"Must have been better than I realized," Craig said. "Somehow, Ricky managed to get everything all spick and span down there before I had a chance to see it. That's pretty impressive."

"But how?" I asked, scratching at my rigid jawline. "How could he have destroyed so much evidence against him?"

"It's amazing how someone with a little money and wherewithal can get a thing like that done," Craig said.

My forehead wrinkled. "You don't seem all that troubled by this."

"Why am I supposed to lament something I have no control over?" he asked. "Don't worry, I'm not giving up on it all together. But I've got Booker on the run right now, even if he pretends to sit there and give me that cool, collected smile."

"What are you going to do?" I asked.

"I'll figure it out," he said. "I just need to be patient and strike when he's not looking."

"He's got eyes everywhere, from the sounds of it," I said.

"That's my suspicion, too," he said.

I sighed, getting to my feet.

"So, what are your plans for the rest of the day?" he asked.

"I'm going to make dinner for all of us," I said. "I might make extra to take over to Mr. Thompson's."

Craig's gaze hardened. "Barb, I really think you should just – "

"It's only a meal," I said. "Vicky thinks it's a good idea, anyway. She said that if Mr. Thompson really is sick, then this could be a way to alleviate some difficulty in their household. Isn't that a good thing regardless?"

Craig's eyes narrowed, and he sighed somewhat heavily out of his nostrils. "You're pushing your luck, kid."

I smirked. "Haven't heard you say that in a while," I said, whisking my plate over to the sink.

"That's because I thought you grew out of knuckleheaded decisions," he said, coming up beside me and ruffling my hair, just like he used to do when I was a little girl. "But…I guess taking them a meal wouldn't hurt. And it might stop your yapping about Thompson, which I know would be good for both of us."

"Good," I said. "Then how does a nice, big bowl of chili sound?"

3

"You know, I'm glad you told Craig that we were doing this," Vicky said two hours later as she and I tromped down the road heading toward Mr. Thompson's driveway. "I hate the idea of you keeping things from him. The poor man's been through enough in his life."

"He's not as sensitive as you think he is," I said, hoisting the pot of chili further up into my arms with the help of my knee. "He still thinks I'm a kid in a lot of ways, and treats me like it."

"It's because you lived away from him for so long, he can only remember you as a child," Vicky said. "It makes sense, really. It'll take some time for him to see you as anything else."

I rolled my eyes. She might have been right about that.

We started up the drive, which was a lot steeper than ours, since Mr. Thompson's house was on the crest of the small hill that his house had been built on. The whole street had varying heights, but Mr. Thompson's might have been one of the tallest.

The house needed work. The roof sagged near the front of the garage, and some of the singles had blown off after a bad thunderstorm that came through that summer. The white paint on the porch had begun to fade and chip, and one side of the swing hung lower, detached from its chain.

This place has definitely seen better days.

Movement up in one of the front windows caught my eye, and I slowed.

"What's the matter?" Vicky asked, her own steps slowing. "What did you see?"

"A curtain moved," I said, my heart skipping. "He already knows we're here."

"Well then, let's just smile and hope he'll answer the door," Vicky said, putting on a practiced grin.

We stepped up and Vicky, carrying a pie just like she said she would, had a free hand to ring the doorbell.

It seemed like several full minutes passed before

we chanced a look at each other. We had seen movement at the curtain, at least I had, but no one was coming to answer?

With wordless agreement, she reached out and rang the bell again.

We heard it echo inside the house, and soon the chime faded into silence.

"I wonder why they don't want to answer," I said.

"I have no idea," Vicky said. She reached out and rapped on the door with her knuckles. *Knock knock knock.* "Mr. Thompson? Hello? It's Vicky Foster and Barbara Hollis. We're just here to bring you some – "

The door flew open with a pulling gust of wind, and the face of Gerald Thompson glared out at us.

Middle-aged and balding, Gerald was not the picture of health. His eyes, gaunt and dark, stared out at us through a pair of wide-framed glasses. "You don't have to yell," he said quietly, cutting Vicky off. "What do you want?"

Vicky gave him one of her million dollar smiles. "Hi, Gerald. We're here to bring you and your father some food." She held out the pie as if to make her point for her, or maybe to entice him a little.

"Yes," I said, lifting the pot up a bit, but it was hard to do as heavy as it was. "We thought that you would both like something warm to eat."

Gerald stared between us, his eyes growing wide. "Why?"

"We haven't seen your father in some time," I said. "We usually see him out on the porch in his rocker – "

"Or taking his morning walk," Vicky added. "We've been worried that he could have gotten sick."

Gerald's mouth opened, and he glanced back and forth between us like we might have something on our faces.

"So…has he?" I asked.

Gerald said nothing, just stared at me.

My eyes narrowed and I looked more closely at him. "Uh…Gerald? Did you hear me?"

He blinked suddenly, shaking his head. "Sorry," he said. "I haven't – slept much lately."

Vicky took a step forward. "Then why don't you just let us bring these inside and put them down for you?" she asked.

"We'd like to see your father, too," I said. "Maybe we can help – "

"No!" Gerald exclaimed, pulling the door closed more tightly against his shoulder, blocking our view any further into the house. "No, it's fine. I can – I can take the food."

I didn't like the tone in his voice, or the somewhat wild look in his eyes. His pupils were like pinpricks, and his tongue passed over his dry lips.

"How is your father?" Vicky asked. "Is it – Oh, bless him, is it serious? He was so worried about his doctor's appointment some months ago – "

"I don't want to talk about it," Gerald said.

"Well, we still need to put all this down," I said. "It's getting kind of heavy."

"Then let me get it," he said, reaching for the pot.

"I should do it," I said. "I just have a few simple instructions for you, how to heat it up, what you should serve it with – "

He took hold of the handles. "I think I can manage whatever it is, just tell me – "

I pulled the pot toward me.

"Oh, really, if you're worried about the house being a mess or anything silly like that, then don't worry," Vicky said, trying to push the door open past him.

"No!" he cried out, pushing her arm from the door, strengthening his hold by placing his foot behind it, barring her from entering. "No, the house – is fine. That's not the problem."

"Then what is the problem?" I asked. "You seem so upset, Gerald. All we want to do is help, all right?"

He looked between us, his face falling. "I…I am just doing this to protect my father."

Protect your father? Or protect yourself?

There was something in the way his eyes winced ever so slightly when he said the word *father*. Like he was anticipating a strike across the face.

"So, everything is fine, then?" I asked.

"You two are both all right?" Vicky asked.

"Y – Yes," he answered. He drew in a deep, steadying breath and looked at his scuffed shoes. "It's been…a rough few weeks. I can't say much, he – he wouldn't want me to. He's proud – and doesn't want pity. Never has."

He wouldn't meet our eyes when he said these things, instead focusing on the faded welcome mat beneath our feet.

"Yes, but even someone as…reclusive as your father deserves to have his neighbors' help and support once in a while," Vicky said kindly. I appreciated the tactfulness of her word choice; I might not have been so thoughtful. "Which is why we wanted to come and alleviate even just one night's worth of meals, in the hopes that it would help you and he out."

He stared at the pie in her hands, turning his gaze up to her. "Is it…pecan?"

She grinned, her face as beautiful as it always was. "It certainly is," she said. "My grandmother's recipe."

Gerald swallowed hard. "Dad's favorite."

"I know!" she said with a laugh. "I remember him saying something about it one time, and I had an extra one in my freezer. They're Robert's favorite, and my oldest child absolutely loves to help me make them whenever we have the pecans floating around the house – "

He shook his head again, as if ridding himself from a reverie. "I – Thanks, but I think I'm – I think we're okay – "

"Please, Gerald," I said, looking pointedly at him. "I made an extra batch of chili especially to bring over here. Just let us give this to you." I hoped he could hear the tone in my voice, asking him *really* what this was all about, giving him permission to be honest with us.

This really had nothing to do with the chili. We both knew that.

He looked lost, like an abandoned dog trying to find his way home.

The debate showed clear on his face, with a flash of fear in his grey eyes. "I – " he said, looking away again. "I'm sorry, I cannot let you in. It's – I just can't."

Vicky sighed, looking at me.

This did not seem to be going our way. Not only that, but he seemed so torn. It was clear something was bothering him, right at the tip of his tongue, but he didn't know whether or not he should say anything to us.

Come on, Gerald. You can talk to us. You can tell us what's happening.

His eyes grew wider, and he shook his head. "No. I'm sorry. Thank you – thank you for the meal, I can't wait to eat it. But I can't let you in. Not right now. Not now."

"...All right," Vicky said, making the decision that I couldn't.

My instincts were frazzled, warning bells going off in my head. The small hairs on the back of my neck were standing straight up. *Something* did not feel right. The house seemed too quiet behind him, like an air of anger and darkness veiled every corner.

"We will leave you to it, then," I said. There really was nothing else I could think to do right now, short of bowling him over. But if old Mr. Thompson was in a foul mood, not expecting guests –

Gerald nodded, and I passed him the pot. He

turned briefly to set it down somewhere out of sight before he turned back to take the pie from Vicky.

In those few seconds while he was turned away, I did my best to peer over his shoulder to see inside. Everything looked dark. I didn't see any light apart from what came through the windows, and the little I could see seemed stagnant.

"I'll...I'll bring back your dishes, when I'm finished," he said.

"That will be just fine," Vicky said. "And, Gerald, if you need anything, please don't hesitate to – "

"I won't," he said, cutting her off. "Need any help, that is."

He started closing the door.

"Goodbye."

He didn't even wait for our answer before he closed the door.

Vicky looked over at me, and I could only sigh.

"Come on."

We headed back down the drive, and neither of us said anything until we were part way up my driveway a few minutes later.

"Well...what do you think?" she asked, lowering her voice as we approached my front door.

I didn't answer until we were inside the house

with the door closed behind us. At least now we could be sure that no one would overhear us.

I let out another sigh.

"That bad, huh?" she asked.

"I need coffee," I said, and started for the kitchen.

"But what do you think?" she asked again, following after me.

"I think he was lying to us," I said, grabbing the percolator and setting it down on the stovetop.

"I guess that much was obvious," she said. "What do you suppose he was lying about?"

"I don't know," I said. "He didn't say nearly enough to be able to figure that out."

"He seemed nervous," she said.

"Which makes me wonder…why?" I asked.

She frowned, folding her arms and crossing them over her chest. "Well…one maybe obvious answer would be that he would have been nervous to meet us regardless of what we thought. He might just be like his father; doesn't like people or know how to interact with them."

"I can imagine that is true, but…" I said, grabbing a fresh, vacuum-sealed coffee from the pantry. This called for the big guns, my favorite blend. "There's something else going on over there. Something that…should I even say it?"

"What? What?" she asked.

"I think something has scared him."

Her eyes widened, and she straightened up. "Scared? Like what?"

"I don't know," I said. "But you were the one telling me that he seemed guilty about something earlier."

"Yes, guilty, but scared?" she asked. "That seems like it might be a bit of a stretch, right? Maybe we are seeing what we want to instead of what we should be?"

"Possibly, but I don't think so..." I said. "Although..."

"What?"

I pursed my lips, eyeing the percolator. "Craig told me that I might be jumping at shadows," I said. "That all these investigations have me looking, like you said, for something that's not there." I frowned. "Maybe bringing a meal over wasn't the best idea."

"Hold on," she said, raising a hand. "I don't know if this is one of those times. I was the one who thought something was wrong this afternoon. You just went along with it."

"But we didn't find out anything," I said. "Just... that something didn't seem right."

"It seemed quiet," she said. "Too quiet."

"I know," I said. The same chill that ran down my back when I was standing in front of Mr. Thompson's house came back to me. "I wonder if Gerald's afraid of his father in some way."

Her eyes grew wide. "You don't suppose...?"

"I half expected to hear the old man's growling shout from the other side of the house, telling him to make us go away," I said.

"Me too!" she exclaimed. "Is he threatening his son in some way?"

"I don't know," I said. "But it's almost like – like Gerald feels trapped. Like he was pleading with us to help, but he couldn't tell us."

"Maybe his father would have overheard," she said.

"That's true," I said. "He didn't say whether or not his father had fallen ill. If he had, then it might be very serious. Who knows what that might make him act like."

She nodded. "This does seem to add up..." she said. "Oh, if only we had been able to get in there and see what was happening. Maybe see his father. I think we would have been able to understand it all a bit more clearly."

"There are so many questions...and visiting him did not alleviate a single one of them," I said. I set the percolator back down on the counter, heaving a sigh. "Craig is not going to be happy with me, but I think it might be time to send him and Roger in."

"Really? On what grounds?" she asked.

I looked at her, my heart sinking. "If there is any sort of abuse happening in that household, then this does actually fall into police territory. Craig didn't want to get involved before, saying that families need to work their issues out themselves, and reluctantly, I do agree with him. This, however, feels...different."

"It certainly seems like there's something wrong over there," she said, then she shivered. "It felt... creepy, almost. I am sorry, Barbara, but if we are handing the reins over to your brother and his deputy, then I might sit the rest of this out. I don't want to put my family in any sort of danger, you know? We're neighbors with the Thompsons, and even though I want to see the matter resolved – "

"You don't have to apologize," I said. "I completely understand. Actually, your reasoning for wanting to step down is the reason I want to be a part of fixing this. They are our neighbors, you're right. I want to help Craig make sure that it's safe... for all of us here."

She nodded. "So, now what?"

"Now, we call my brother," I said, starting out through the kitchen doorway to the phone. But I paused, mid-step. "Come to think of it, I should probably go down to the station and talk to Craig in person to make sure he understands the importance. Then, he and Roger can be the ones to kick in the door."

"Kick in the door?" she exclaimed. "Barb, I don't think it's that pressing."

"I know that," I said. "But after I tell Craig what we saw, he might just be willing to do that. He might have no choice."

4

I never knew that the inside of a building could be so cold.

Vicky and I stepped inside what felt like an ice box, both of us drawing our coats further up our shoulders, pulling them tightly closed around our middles.

"Does this place not have any sort of heating?" I asked as I passed straight by the receptionist's desk – not that it mattered, since she was hardly ever there these days.

Vicky stayed close behind me, her eyes wide as we circled around the still empty cubicle area between the front of the station and the offices where Craig and Elwood worked.

"Tell me again why you insisted I come with you?" she asked.

"Because he will need to hear this from the both of us, not just me," I said. "Otherwise he might not believe me at all and just tell me to go home."

Vicky looked warily at me.

"I know you don't want to be involved in this anymore, and I completely understand that," I said. "This is the last thing I'll ask of you."

"All right," she said. "Thank you."

Grateful that she didn't doubt me, I strode up to Craig's office door and gave it a sharp knock. We only had to wait a few seconds before he called us inside. He knew it was us coming, since the whole front wall of his office was made up entirely of windows.

"Hey, what's happening?" he asked as we stepped inside.

"I'm glad we caught you here," I said. "I didn't like the idea of having to drive all over creation just to find you."

His smile faltered a bit as he sat up in his chair.

"What's up, boss?"

I turned to see Roger Elwood slip into the room behind us. I arched an eyebrow at him.

"Don't give me that look," he said. "I see you're here, I know there's trouble."

I opened my mouth to retort, but Craig stepped in.

"Oh, please, don't tell me that's why you're here," Craig said, laying his head in his hand. "I feel like I'm just getting things under control around here. I don't have time to deal with anything else."

"Well, I hate to be the bearer of bad news, but there's definitely something going on at the Thompson household," I said.

Craig lowered his hand, but kept it firmly across the lower half of his face, eyeing me with disbelief.

"Isn't that your crazy coot of a neighbor?" Roger asked. "The one that lives right next door?"

"Yes..." Craig said between his fingers. "I take it that you ladies went over there like you said you were going to?"

I nodded.

He leaned forward in his seat. "But you promised me you weren't going to do anything funny," he said. "You promised me you would stay out of whatever it is."

"Yes, well, Gerald Thompson's made it pretty clear that there's something going on there," I said.

"Like what?" Craig asked, resting his elbows on his desk.

I crossed my arms. "He didn't say, exactly."

Craig rolled his eyes, falling back against his chair.

"But there's obviously something wrong," I said. "That's why I brought Vicky with me, so you wouldn't treat me like an imbecile."

"Nobody has said you're an – " he started, then groaned.

Roger came to stand beside Craig at his desk. He looked like a bodyguard, standing there with his broad shoulders and checkered, flannel shirt.

"Look, all I know is that either Mr. Thompson is harming his son, or his son is keeping his father locked up tight," I said.

"Whoa, that's quite the accusation," Roger said, even as Craig's mouth fell open. "Do you have any proof to back up that sort of claim?"

"You wouldn't think it was so crazy if you saw Gerald's face," Vicky said. "He looked...lost. Vacant."

"He always looks like that," Craig said, clearly trying to gather himself.

"He looked like he wanted to tell us something, but just couldn't bring himself to do it," I said. "He said he couldn't talk about his father, that his father wouldn't want pity."

"He's a proud man, yes, I know that," Craig said. "But why do you think Gerald is the one being abused?"

"I don't know if he is," I said. "He just looked… afraid. And you told me that you've had to deal with these sorts of situations and the person who was being threatened was always too afraid to say anything, even if it could get them help."

"And he wouldn't give us any sort of answer about his father," Vicky said. "Which worried me because I usually see him every day, out on the porch, in the front drive, digging through the flower beds in the yard." She shook her head. "I can't remember the last time I saw him, but it hasn't been for several weeks now."

Craig sighed. "Yet neither of you have any answers," he said. He glowered at me. "Barbara, I told you, this is not the sort of situation that we can interfere with. There isn't anything dangerous going on – "

"Now, just hold on…"

It was Roger who spoke, which surprised me.

Craig looked up over his shoulder at his deputy. "What? Don't tell me you're agreeing with her?"

"Well…you and I both know that it happens more regularly than we would like that when we feel like something's amiss, it's because it typically is."

Craig shook his head. "I know this man. I know this family. I've lived next to them for years. Why won't anyone listen to me about this?"

"I've lived near him, too," Vicky said. "And ordinarily, I'd agree with you. But there was definitely something…funny about the way that Gerald was acting. I don't know if it was shame or fear or maybe both that kept him from letting us speak with his father, but I'm a little worried for both of them."

"If there is something going wrong in that house, something that could become dangerous, then we do have an obligation to step in," Roger said. "Think of your boys. What if one of the Thompsons lashes out when they're nearby? What if a gun is involved? What if they're out in the backyard and – "

Craig raised a hand, and shot Roger a quelling look.

Roger shut his mouth obediently. I had to give him credit for standing his ground and yet still respecting my brother.

"…All right," Craig said, pointing a finger right at me, then shifting it to Vicky. "But only because *you* came, too. You would know as well as I would when something was amiss. If there's anything going wrong, then we have an obligation to check on it. Roger's right about that."

"Thank you," Vicky said. "This whole thing's had me worried sick all day, and I know that Robert will be eternally grateful when I tell him everything you've done."

Craig got to his feet, shuffling some papers aside. "Yes, well, hopefully I can tell him myself, and it won't be anything important."

The two men pulled on their coats, armed themselves, and got into Craig's police car. Vicky hopped back into my truck with me, and we headed back toward Pine Street.

Craig pulled his car to a stop in our driveway, and as Vicky and I were getting out of the truck, he wandered over. "Now, Roger and I have come to a decision, and I think it's the best one. We want you ladies to stay back here at the house, just in case something goes wrong."

I opened my mouth to argue, but Vicky grabbed hold of my arm, shaking her head.

"He's right," she said. "If things really are as tense as they felt like they were when we were there, then it's best if the police go in without our weight. They're prepared to handle this." She eyed Craig's belt holster which remained out of sight, hidden beneath his jacket.

I pursed my lips. "Okay."

"We won't tell them that you two were the ones who tipped us off, either," he said.

"Craig, of course they're going to know that it was us," I said. "We only just left an hour ago."

"We aren't going to say anything about what you told us," Roger said, coming up beside Craig. "Just that we'd heard that there might be someone hurt or injured inside, and we wanted to come see if there was any truth to any of it before we called the hospital."

"And what if he tells you 'no' like he told us?" I asked.

"Barb, I already told you that we can't push this," Craig said. "We can't force anyone to tell us what is going on in their family. Maybe the pair of them are just having a fight over something right now. Maybe someone else in the household has gotten sick. There are a lot of possible explanations for Gerald's behavior."

"I know that," I snapped. "It just...didn't feel right. All the hairs on my neck stood up."

Roger raised his eyebrows, looking at Craig.

Craig nodded. "Roger's willing to listen to you this time, so I am, too," he said.

I glared at Roger. "That's suspiciously nice of you."

He shrugged. "I'm starting to learn that you aren't always full of it, and this time, you definitely weren't pulling Craig's leg. You are genuinely worried, and I think that's a good enough reason to look. If it's nothing, it's nothing, and we can move on. If it is something, well, then you might have saved someone."

Might have saved someone. Another shiver passed over me as I looked up at him. I hated to think that his words of praise might end up proving true, but if they did...then it really was for the best that Vicky and I had said something, wasn't it?

"Okay, you two stay here," Craig said. "We'll go see what's going on."

The two men sauntered down the driveway and down the street, both in their brown, flat-brimmed hats. They looked like an intimidating pair.

"I wonder what Mr. Thompson is going to think when he sees these two coming..." I said.

"Probably confusion," Vicky said. "And either relief, or terror. I'm not sure which is the better option, really."

She and I decided the porch would be the best viewing platform, the swing having an almost clear view of the yard next door. The wood creaked beneath us as we swung gently back and forth, the pillows faded from months out in the sunshine.

My heart beat uncomfortably in my chest as I watched them approach the front door. I pulled a knee up onto the swing, trying to look relaxed for Vicky's sake, but her own eyes were glued unblinkingly across the way, too.

Roger knocked first, then stepped back.

It couldn't have been more then five seconds later that the door opened, and Gerald's pale face appeared.

"That was fast," I said. "He must have seen them coming."

"He probably didn't think it would be very smart to keep the police waiting at the door," Vicky said. "Oh, why am I so nervous?"

I was nervous, too, but I didn't want her to panic. I hadn't really considered all the possibilities of what might happen when they were to actually go up to the door. *This is how some police officers lose their lives, walking up to dangerous situations like this.*

My heart raced, the blood pounding in my ears.

"It'll be fine," I said, just as much for Vicky as for myself. "He didn't attack us this morning; I can't imagine he'd be foolish enough to do anything to them."

Sure enough, Gerald stepped aside, and with a sweeping motion, appeared to invite Craig and Roger inside.

Vicky and I both sat up straight, staring in surprise.

"Did he – let them in?" I asked.

"I think he did," she said. "But – why?"

I felt a twinge of relief. "I guess...they have more authority then we do, obviously. Maybe seeing them spooked both him and his dad."

"I wouldn't refuse a policeman wanting to come and check on me," Vicky said. "I'd do everything I could to assuage his concerns."

She and I looked at one another. That was *mostly* true, seeing how she and I had worked together to destroy any evidence of a case she had testified in years ago by setting her garden storage shed on fire. It had been mostly me, but she never told a soul what had happened.

We stared at the front door to Mr. Thompson's house for what felt like an eternity, even though nothing happened. The wind blew, the trees danced, but still neither Craig nor Roger came back out of that house.

"How long do you think they're going to stay in there?" Vicky asked.

It was difficult to know just how much time had passed. It might have been two or three minutes, or it might have been fifteen. "I don't know," I said. "All I can hope is that we won't have to go over there and find out."

Vicky shuddered next to me, glancing across the street at her house.

"If you want to head home, I would understand –"

"And leave you here all by yourself? No," she said flatly, shaking her head. "Besides, I'd be agonizing over this there, too. The kids won't be home for a little while. I can stay with you at least until then."

"Thank you," I said. I didn't really know what I'd do when she left if they still hadn't come out yet.

It's unlikely that nothing will happen in the next hour, I told myself, reassured myself. *They'll probably reappear soon enough, and –*

Even before the thoughts had fully formed in my mind, movement at the door caused me to jump off the swing and hurry to the edge of the porch.

With bated breath, I stared at Mr. Thompson's

door, and sagged with relief as Craig and Roger strode casually back outside.

"Okay..." I breathed, squeezing the railing with white knuckles. "Okay, everything's fine."

Vicky nodded, but she'd definitely lost some of the color in her cheeks.

I couldn't make out their faces from as far away as we were, so we had to wait the agonizing minute and a half it would take them to get back over to our house.

"What do you think happened?" Vicky asked in a low murmur.

"I have no idea," I said. I stared at the door, but it had already closed again. "I didn't even see who it was that let them out."

"Do you think – do you think it's possible that we were just overreacting?" she asked.

I didn't know how to answer. "I hope so," I said, and yet somehow felt unsatisfied with that idea. I *knew* something was wrong. Maybe I was a little too sensitive to it and it was the sort of problem that I had no business knowing about, but that didn't mean I was wrong...

...Did it?

I had to restrain myself from hurrying down to the end of the driveway as Craig and Roger came to it. I didn't want Mr. Thompson or Gerald to look out the window and see me frantic and scurrying about.

"Well?" I called, waiting until I only had to raise my voice slightly to be heard over the windy, afternoon chill.

Craig said nothing, but gave me a look as he and Roger practically meandered their way up the drive.

I stared at him, waiting for an answer –

"Inside," Craig said, and he let the four of us in.

Indoors, I had barely turned around when he spoke again.

"There's nothing going on, Barb."

I stared at him, licking my dry lips. I turned my gaze to Roger.

He shrugged, but nodded his head. "He's telling you the truth."

Craig's eyes narrowed and he looked between the pair of us. "Since when are you taking her side in these things?"

Again, Roger shrugged.

"What happened?" Vicky asked. "You were gone for some time."

"Well, Gerald met us at the door," Craig said. "He seemed a little surprised to see us, wouldn't you say, Roger?"

"More than a little," Roger said. "But we

explained to him that some people in the neighborhood were getting a little concerned about his father, having not seen him for some time. He laughed and said that he could understand why. His father had become sensitive to the cold these days, and hadn't really wanted to venture outside much."

"He welcomed us in, told us that we were free to look around," Craig said.

"Did you see old Mr. Thompson?" I asked.

"No," Craig said.

"But Gerald told us before we even asked that his father had stepped out because one of his friends from Reddington had come to pick him up for the rest of the day. He wasn't really sure where they were going, but he assumed it might have just been for a drive to get him out of the house."

"You're kidding..." I said, looking over at Vicky.

She had a hand over her heart, and she looked immensely relieved.

I, however, wasn't so easily convinced. "Then why didn't Gerald just *tell* us any of this?"

"I told you, he and his father are strange," Craig said. "He was odd with us, too. Uncomfortable."

"And that didn't worry you?" I asked.

"How so?" Craig asked. "He let us in, let us look around. Guilty people don't do that."

"Unless he planned to let you do that so you'd believe him," I said.

Craig shook his head. "Barbara, listen to yourself for a second. You *want* there to be something wrong. You got a taste of investigative work and now you want more of it."

I blushed scarlet. "I do not want any of that!"

"Who knows why he might have been acting a little odd this morning," Roger said. "Maybe they had a fight, maybe his father was acting up again."

"It could have been anything you can think of," Craig said.

"We gave the whole house a quick walk through," Roger said. "His invitation inside was his way of trying to show, in good faith, that he was telling the truth. And there was evidence of his father being there recently. We saw laundry out back on the line, and I noticed his medicine on the sink in the bathroom with half a glass of water beside it."

I didn't quite know what to say. If his things were out around the house, then it was easier to believe Gerald was telling the truth.

I turned to look at Vicky, whose eyes were still a little wide.

"What do you think?"

"I'm relieved," she said. "In fact, I think I can head home now...if it's all right with you."

I couldn't tell if she was upset with me. "I'm sorry for wasting your time today," I said.

She shook her head. "No, I'm the one who made you worry in the first place."

"Right..." I said.

She started toward the door, and gave me a smile. "Honestly, I'm glad. Thank you, Sheriff, and Deputy, for going and looking into this for us."

"You're quite welcome," Roger said, bowing his head.

"Say hello to Robert for me," Craig said as she left.

Then he turned to me. The both of them did, like I was some child about to be told that Santa Claus wasn't real. Not in trouble, but pitiable.

"Don't let this eat at you, okay?" Craig asked, shrugging his coat off. It looked like he planned to stay home the rest of the day. He might as well, given that it was already late in the afternoon.

"I can see why you thought there was something strange about them," Roger said.

"That's very charitable of you," I said, but couldn't help let him hear some of the venom in my heart.

He smirked at me.

"I think your heart is in the right place," Craig said, coming to lay a hand on my shoulder. "You might think that Mr. Thompson is a crotchety old man like I do, but you still want to make sure everyone is all right."

I looked away. That might be true.

"This sort of sensitivity is normal when you've been involved in unraveling dangerous situations recently," Roger said. "Some people think they need to save everyone from everything. Their nerves are turned way up, and they don't really remember what it's like for people to behave normally, even in the middle of fights and other difficulties."

I nodded. "That makes sense," I said.

"Why don't we just agree to let it go, say that we did a good deed for the day?" Craig asked. He didn't wait for my answer, heading for the kitchen. "Roger, you want to stay for dinner tonight?"

"Sure, sounds good to me," Roger said, sliding his hands into his pockets. He looked at me. "As long as Barbara doesn't mind having another mouth to feed."

I sighed, starting after Craig. "It's fine. I made enough to feed an army as it is."

While they dug through the ice box to find the

sweet tea, I set the large pot of chili back onto the stove to warm up.

I didn't know why I felt disappointed. It was the ideal outcome to what had seemed like a tense situation. It could have been so much worse. While it was happening, I feared the worst for Craig, wondering if I'd sent him to his death. In the dark recesses of my mind, I was already trying to figure out exactly how I would explain what happened to Toby and Tim.

That stress, that worry, had all been a waste.

Wasn't that a good thing? Shouldn't I feel relieved?

Why didn't I feel relieved?

I gave the cooled chili a mix with a wooden spoon while Craig and Roger shared a laugh about something behind me. I might as well have tried mixing drying cement.

Roger's concern returned to me. *Some people think they need to save everyone from everything.*

Is that all this was? Had I become overly sensitive? Had I forgotten what normal life was really like?

I shook my head, unwilling to even consider the possibility. No, I was fine. Everything was fine.

5

I slammed a fist against the cold, hard side of the sink in the bathroom.

"Ow..." I said, shaking my hand. *That was stupid.*

It worked, though. It cleared my thoughts some.

I had been wandering around the house like I was half asleep all day, unable to fully draw my mind out of the dream that had been plaguing me since it had woken me at four in the morning.

I swallowed hard, staring at my reflection in the toothpaste spattered mirror.

The corridor hadn't been what troubled me. It had been long, never ending, and I couldn't really remember where it had started or where I was heading to. The same dull, fading wallpaper followed me as I walked. There were no doors, apart from the one at the very end. The one I couldn't reach.

What had troubled me so much...what still haunted me was the voice.

Mr. Thompson's voice.

I'd heard him laugh, which I really couldn't ever remember hearing in real life, but then he started sobbing. Then he would laugh again. Cry. Laugh.

I didn't understand it.

It had been almost a week since the incident, as I'd been calling it in my mind. Craig and I had said nothing else about it. He hadn't asked, and neither had I. I'd told him and Roger that I would let it go.

Vicky had managed to let it go. Why was it that I couldn't? She had thought that Craig and Roger's examination of everything had been thorough enough. Why was it that I could only see the fear in Gerald's eyes when we had spoken with him at the door?

I switched on the tap in the bathroom, waiting until it was just hot enough for me to stand it, and plunged my hands underneath.

I really needed to get a hold of myself.

I had started to consider that maybe the issue really was me. I didn't know if I was getting enough sleep. I didn't know if I had started eating something that was not agreeing with me. My whole life had been upended when I moved here, and I was starting to wonder if it was only now just catching up with me.

I found it extremely difficult to place the source of my trouble squarely on my own shoulders. Everything within me fought the idea; *No, it can't be me. It must be something outside of me. I haven't changed, have I? There isn't some foundational problem that needs to be addressed. I'm perfectly fine. I'm fine!*

I splashed some of the water up onto my face, and while I would have liked nothing more than to submerge myself into an entire tub full of it, I had other things I needed to take care of at the moment. More important matters.

Leaving the bathroom, I exhaled all the frustrations and smiled as I stepped out into the living room where the twins were waiting.

Tim lay stretched out on the couch, a book spread across the cushion in front of him while his brother lounged in front of the television on his belly, feet kicking lazily into the air behind him.

"Well, aren't you both a sight to behold?" I asked, reaching behind me to tighten the straps of my apron. "First day of Christmas vacation and you're already lying here like a couple of bears in hibernation."

Toby rolled over onto his side and grinned up at me. "We've earned it. You have no idea how hard that math test was yesterday."

Tim glanced up from his book. "Isn't this what Christmas vacation should look like?"

I laughed. "Of course it is. However, you two *did* promise me that you'd help me make some cookies."

The *click* of the television power switch narrowly beat the *clap* of Tim's book snapping shut. The two scrambled to their feet, standing in front of me with their arms pressed together.

I smirked, looking between them with my hands on my hips. "Well, don't you look like a pair of soldiers? All right then, troops, we've got about six or seven dozen cookies to bake, and no time to lose! Tim, get the flour and the sugar. Toby, the chocolate chips and the oatmeal."

"Right!" they exclaimed, and tripped over each other as they turned to scurry ahead of me like a pack of hunting dogs having caught the scent.

I smiled, shaking my head.

A loud *thunk* sent my heart racing, and I jumped, letting out a yelp of surprise.

Toby's face reappeared, eyes wide. "What is it?"

I stood there in the middle of the living room, hand on my heart. "It's okay, just the newspaper," I said. "I'll get it."

He nodded and disappeared. Somewhere from the other side of the doorway, I heard a *thud,* followed by an, "Uh oh – Everything's fine!"

I pulled open the door and caught sight of Phillip on his bike just as he passed by in front of Vicky and Robert's house across the street, on his way back up Pine Street. I shook my head. Since he took over the paper route from Steven, not only had our papers been arriving later, but the deliveries were a great deal less ceremonious –

Gerald appeared at the end of his driveway, dressed in a deep blue bathrobe, with his arms wrapped tightly around himself for warmth. It seemed Phillip hadn't managed to get his paper all that far up the driveway. Inconsistent *and* indifferent. Not a great combination.

I stood there for a moment, watching Gerald stoop to pick up the newspaper.

I frowned. *Only one newspaper?*

Mr. Thompson always had two papers; one was the regular paper, and the other was the specialty book of crosswords they delivered every Saturday. Craig had gotten it a few times but quickly stopped it. He said he hardly had time to do one of them, let alone a book of ten or twelve of them. It was easily distinguishable for its green cover, and it was usually wrapped around the regular newspaper.

The paper Gerald held looked the same as mine. No green to be seen.

That's odd.

I frowned. Why was it that I couldn't seem to ignore any of this?

Tucking the paper underneath my arm, I headed back inside.

This was not the first time I'd seen Gerald since Craig and Roger had walked through the Thompson house. I'd seen him taking the trash out again, going to get the mail from the mailbox, even once getting into his car and driving away somewhere. I'd debated about getting into my truck and going after him, but I knew that I really needed to let this go.

Everyone else had.

For some reason, though, Gerald had taken over the tasks that Mr. Thompson used to do...and once again, I began to wonder if Mr. Thompson had gotten sick. It must have been something severe to have him cooped up the way he seemed to be.

Then how could he have had the energy to go out for a drive with his friend last week?

I shook my head, shutting the door behind me.

I would not let this get to me. I wouldn't. Craig was right; it was their business, not mine.

Smiling once again, I headed into the kitchen where the boys were.

"Anything good?" Toby asked.

"No idea," I said, tossing it onto the counter. "Your father will have to look it over to know."

"Where's the recipe?" Tim asked, pulling one of the mixing bowls from one of the lower cupboards.

"Hold on," I said, retrieving a cookbook from the top shelf of the pantry.

"How old is that?" Toby asked, his brows wrinkling together. "Looks like it must be from a hundred years ago."

I shot him a look, a brow arched. "Older than you, that's for sure. Older than your dad. This belonged to my grandmother. She handwrote a lot of these recipes, including the cookie recipe that you boys love so much, or so I've been told."

Toby gave me a wry smile and said nothing more.

We set about getting all the ingredients together, even though Toby complained that he just wanted to start. I promised him that he'd have cookies within the hour, but that didn't stop him from throwing his head back and groaning.

I tossed a set of tin measuring spoons at him. "You know, I might not have known you when you were younger, but I can't be that far off to assume that this was how you acted when you were a toddler."

Toby gaped at me while Tim snickered at the cookbook, pouring over the recipe that I'd turned to.

"Let's turn on the radio," I said, reaching over to flip on the switch of the radio Craig kept in the kitchen. Sometimes, on the weekends, he liked to leave it on all day so that whenever he passed in and out of the kitchen, working on projects and making breakfast and lunch for all of us, he'd catch snatches of his favorite Bing Crosby songs.

"That's better," I said, as a Christmas song filled the room.

I hated that I wasn't enjoying this as much as I should have been. I'd been looking forward to baking Gram's cookies with the boys for the past two months. I had wanted to surprise Craig with a house full of them so that when he got home, it not only smelled heavenly but he'd have cookies to eat all through the weeks leading up to Christmas itself. I had plans for hot cocoa, for mulled cider, for pies and roasts and –

The telephone started to ring.

Tim glanced up at me. He'd already started to measure out the sugar for the cookies, having set a spoon against the page to prevent it from closing on him.

I sighed. *Just when I was trying to get into the Christmas spirit...*

"I can get it," Toby said.

"Go ahead," I answered.

Toby darted out of the kitchen.

"Now...let's see, we need about a cup and a half of butter for these. If we want to double the recipe... I don't know if we have enough butter, if I'm honest," I said.

"That's okay, let's try the recipe and see how it turns out," Tim said,

"Good idea," I said. "I haven't made these in a while, and without your dad's expertise, I can't guarantee that these won't turn out horribly wrong."

Tim smiled up at me. "Don't worry, Aunt Barbara. I think I can help you make sure they don't get messed up too badly."

"Thanks," I said. "Now, where'd I put the – "

"Aunt Barbara? It's Mrs. Foster!" Toby called from the other room.

"Okay, I'm coming," I said. "I'll be back in a minute, Tim. Don't get too far along without me; I want to help!"

"You got it," Tim said, dipping the measuring cup into the tub of sugar.

Wiping my hands on my apron, I hurried out to the phone table where Toby stood, holding the receiver. He smiled as he passed it to me.

"Thanks," I said.

He nodded, and went to join Tim in the kitchen.

"Hello, Vicky," I said, brushing from my eyes a few stray hairs that had fallen out of the bandana I'd tied my hair back with. "How's it going?"

"Oh, it's going great!" she said. "We got our tree, finally! Robert has been so busy with work that we hadn't been able to find a good night to go and get one, but we finally did!"

"That's wonderful!" I said, turning to look out the window and down the yard toward her house. "I can't wait to see it!"

"It's nothing to behold right now, but we will probably spend a good amount of time on it tonight when they all get back – they went Christmas shopping for me today, all together. Isn't that sweet?"

"It's adorable," I said. "You're home by yourself, then?"

"Yes, for now," she said.

"You want to come over? The twins and I were just about to start making cookies."

"No, that's okay, there was just something I wanted to share with you," she said, and some of the brightness in her tone faded.

"Uh oh," I said. "What's the matter?"

"Nothing's the matter. I just…thought you should know." I heard paper crinkling in the background. "Sorry, I'm trying to get some of the kids' presents wrapped while they aren't home. I just wanted you to know that my brother-in-law and his family were over for dinner last night, and he told us an…well, an interesting story."

I leaned against the phone table, tucking my free hand beneath my arm. "You say interesting like it's a bad thing," I said.

"Not bad, I guess, just…interesting," she said.

"Well, don't keep me in suspense here, Vicky. Tell me what happened."

"My husband's brother owns the drug store downtown," Vicky said. "Family business for years, their father owned it and then it was passed to my brother-in-law – "

"Yes, Vicky, you've told me that before," I said. "Not to be rude, but is it relevant?"

"Sort of," she said. "I'm sorry, I didn't know if I should even call and tell you this, but something told me I should. Anyway, we were sitting down to dinner last night, and Neil told us that he had the most bizarre interaction with a customer that day. He's a pharmacist, remember, and so he sees people from the town pretty regularly. I'd argue that he knows everyone about as well as your brother does."

"I'm sure he does," I said. I had a sneaking suspicion I knew the direction this was heading.

"He said that he was busy getting some peppermint sticks made up for an order when a middle-aged man came into the drug store," she said. "He came right up to the counter and asked if he could speak with the pharmacist. My brother-in-law told him that he had already found him and was speaking with him. He tried to make it a joke, but the man at the counter didn't find it humorous, I guess. Neil's a really funny guy, so it surprised him that someone seemed so stiff."

"You've said as much," I said. "So, who was this man?"

"Hang on, I'm getting there," Vicky said.

I tried to resist the urge to snap at her to hurry

up; I knew how much Vicky liked to tell stories, and she hardly ever talked just to hear the sound of her own voice. There was a reason behind why she was taking the long way around to tell me what she wanted to.

"This man had apparently brought some medications back to the drug store," she said. "To return them."

My brow furrowed. "Is that even possible?"

"Not really, no," Vicky said. "I said that I had never heard of anyone doing that, and Neil said neither had he! Well, he apparently tried to make a joke with the man, asking if he'd somehow gotten the wrong order, maybe the wrong number of doses? The man simply shook his head and said that he was simply there to bring back medications that were for his father."

I knew *exactly* where this was going, now. "I can see why your brother-in-law thought to share that with you and Robert," I said. "It is out of the ordinary."

"He said he'd never seen anything like it," Vicky agreed. "He recognized the name on the glass bottle that the man handed over to him. It was an order for an elderly customer who faithfully came in every four weeks to pick up a new bottle. It wasn't as if the customer needed it to survive, nothing quite so serious Neil said, but he said that it was prepared especially to help him with pain and swelling joints in his legs."

"Oh, dear..." I said, shaking my head.

Vicky went on. "The son firmly told Neil that his father no longer had need of the medication and asked for his money back for this particular batch. Neil explained to him as best he could that it was not the store's policy to give refunds for such particular medicines, and the man left annoyed."

"And the man was Gerald Thompson?" I asked.

"Precisely my thought," Vicky said. "I asked Neil who he was, but he had trouble remembering the man's name. Even though his father came in every month, he couldn't remember the last name...not until I reminded him."

"Oh, boy..." I said. "Did Robert know what you were getting at?"

"He did, because I'd told him everything about what happened that day we went over there," she said. "He thought the whole thing very odd, too. The both of us cannot for the life of us figure out what must be happening with poor old Mr. Thompson."

I sighed, staring out the window toward Vicky's house where she currently sat on her own telephone, mulling over these thoughts with me. "I've begun to worry that he's got some awful disease that makes him either horribly contagious or an invalid," I said. "Either way, it's not good, and his son isn't handling it well."

"No, he's not," Vicky said. "But what if it's not either of those things? What if Gerald has just got his father all cooped up inside for no good reason?"

"Why would he want to stop collecting a medication that's meant to help alleviate some soreness for his father?" I wondered. "It seems like it's more to keep him comfortable than anything else."

"I suppose it could be that he just doesn't need it anymore," Vicky said. "Or maybe it's not helping anymore like it used to. There are a lot of possible explanations as to why…but I didn't really know what to think…which is why I called you."

I chuckled. "Well, I appreciate it, though I'm not really sure that I can help ease any of your confusion."

She sighed heavily, and the *riiip* of scissors through wrapping paper punctuated her point. "I didn't expect you to, but I definitely hoped sharing the information would make me feel better about the whole thing."

"Did it?" I asked warily.

"No," she said. "It didn't. It just frustrated me further because I really was feeling relieved about everything after your brother and his deputy walked through the place..." She sighed again. "I guess I wish they'd had the chance to actually talk to Mr. Thompson instead of just hearing about him second hand through his son."

She hit the nail squarely on the head. "You put into words what I haven't been able to," I said.

Neither of us said anything for a few seconds. "We wanted to let it go. We all agreed, didn't we?" she asked.

"Right," I said. "Which is why I haven't said anything else about this to Craig. I keep seeing Gerald out and about, but I haven't seen Mr. Thompson yet."

"I haven't, either, and I keep looking for him," Vicky said. "Robert said that I'm just getting myself all worked up over nothing, and he's usually right when it comes to my worries."

"Maybe you should listen to him," I said.

"Are you sure?" Vicky asked. "I just – the whole thing – "

"I know," I said. "But we both should let it go. Why does it matter to us what Mr. Thompson chose to do with his medications?"

"It shouldn't," Vicky said. "Normally, I wouldn't care at all. I would have listened to Neil's story and been a little surprised by it, but then I would have had to help the kids get things ready for school the next day or maybe wandered into the kitchen to start cleaning up from dinner. It is only because of the fact that it's Mr. Thompson and everything still seems so…unusual."

"That's a good way of putting it…" I said. "Well, thanks for sharing it with me. I guess in some way there's comfort in the fact that we'll know if anything really bad happens, right? After all, the Thompsons are right next door."

Vicky let out a strangled sort of laugh. "Yes…I guess that's true."

"Try not to worry very much about it," I said. "It's getting so close to Christmas that you shouldn't be thinking about anyone other than your family."

"Barb, the same could be said of you," she said. "Your brother and those boys…they need you. And it's your first Christmas with them since you moved to Cobbsville."

"I know, you're right," I said. "Let's agree again to set this all aside?"

"Agreed," she said. "No more. We'll just let the Thompsons deal with their own problems."

"Exactly. All right, Vicky. I'm going to get back to baking cookies with the twins, okay?"

"You have a wonderful time doing just that," she said. "We're planning to start all that tomorrow. Don't want to leave it 'til the last minute, of course!"

"Oh, are you all still planning to come to the Christmas party at the police station?" I asked.

"We wouldn't miss it for the world," Vicky said brightly.

"Great," I said. "Okay, talk to you soon! Bye!"

"Bye, Barbara!"

I set the phone down, and my smile faded.

It didn't seem to matter what I did.

It wasn't that I was the one unwilling to give up this whole trouble with Mr. Thompson...

No, it was definitely that it didn't seem to want to give up on me.

I tried not to worry over it. I really did. Even just before Vicky called. But how in the world was I supposed to *not* think about it all when it seemed to keep shoving itself in front of my face? It was like being at a peacock exhibit at the zoo and being told to look everywhere but at the glorious, voluminous plumage of the male strutting about his domain.

I made my way back into the kitchen, finding the twins standing at the counter, heads bent together, murmuring to each other. Tim's finger, pressed firmly to the page, traced the cursive handwriting with benevolent care, pausing only if he couldn't quite make out a letter or two.

I stood back, watching them for a few minutes before they discovered me.

"What'd Mrs. Foster want?" Toby asked, turning to me.

"Oh, just to tell me a funny story her brother-in-law told last night over dinner," I said. "Nothing all that important, really."

Toby shrugged, but Tim continued to look at me.

His gaze pierced right through me, and even when I looked away, unable to handle his stare, he still watched me.

He has eyes just like his Dad, but I think he sees through people more deeply than I've ever known some adults to do.

I clapped my hands together, trying to smile again. "All right, then, let's get to work on these," I said. "We've got our work cut out for us today, boys. No sense in wasting time! Let's double up these recipes!"

"But we already started this batch!" Toby complained.

"It doesn't matter, let's just add to it," I said. "Otherwise we are going to be here all day!"

Tim said nothing, only moved over a bit so I could sidle up beside him at the counter.

"Everything all right?" he asked.

"Yes," I said, and then I understood. *He might be able to read that the phone call rattled me, but he has no idea about Mr. Thompson. He must be thinking about something else entirely, probably Vicky's daughter.* "Don't worry. Everything's fine with Elaine Foster."

He went a little red in his ears. "That's not why – "

"It's okay," I said, and smiled at him. "Really. I get it."

I could see him questioning whether or not to trust me, but in the end he must have, because he reached for the wooden spoon and handed it to me. "Thanks," he said as he returned to the cookbook.

I smirked, shaking my head. *Oh, boy...if only you weren't as easy to read as your Dad, I'd say you have a real chance of following in his footsteps.*

Then again, being through everything I'd been through with the deaths and murders and investigations... I really could confidently say that I wouldn't wish that sort of trouble on anyone. Especially not one of my nephews.

Reflecting on the promise I'd made with Vicky, I turned up the Christmas music and rolled up my sleeves. Today was about baking cookies, *not* finding out why Mr. Thompson no longer needed the medicine that he'd been taking for years.

6

One week. There was only one week left until Christmas.

Seven days to clean the house from top to bottom. Seven days to make sure all the clothes for Christmas Eve service were washed, dried, and pressed. Seven days to make sure that I had every present for Craig and the boys. I feared that I had one too many gifts for Toby, or that they might not be equally weighted. The last thing I wanted was to cause a feud between them because they thought that I loved one of them more based on the merit or quality of gifts that I'd gotten for them.

As such, I determined to go back out and look for a few more things for both of them. Craig would have to realize that I planned to spoil them without reason this year. It had been weighing especially hard on me that their mom was gone. I had noticed it before, but this time of year made it apparent like never before. These boys had no mother. I could never replace her, but I could stand in for her. I could only hope that I was doing Becky justice by loving on the twins the way I was trying to, doing as much as I could to make Christmas special again.

It was the least that I could do for them.

I stood in front of my closet, counting on the ends of my fingers. *Four, five – no, wait, I got those books for them, too, so that would still count as five –*

"Hey, Barb?"

I turned to see Craig peeking into my room. Just like when we were kids, he usually gave my room a wide berth, respecting my privacy. As I'd gotten older, though, and moved into his house, I realized that it was just because the idea of walking into a woman's room terrified him, even if it was his own sister's.

I smirked at him, stepping fully in front of the closet, blocking it from his view. "Yes?"

"I'm heading to the station while the boys are over at the Fosters," he said. "Did you need me to pick up anything on my way home?"

"Actually, yes," I said. "I have that red dress over

at the dry cleaner's. If you could grab that, I'd be grateful. I wanted to wear it to the Christmas party at the station."

He nodded. "I'd be happy to. Anything else?"

"No, that's okay," I said. "I need to go to the market to get a few more things myself, so I won't ask you to do that for me."

"All right," he said with a smile. Then his eyes narrowed ever so slightly. "You, uh…you all right?"

"Oh, yes, I'm fine," I said. "Why?"

"I don't know," he said. "You've just seemed… overly determined these last few days to get everything exactly right for Christmas."

I looked around. "Well…yes," I said. "For the boys. I want to try and make my first Christmas with them special."

"Got it," Craig said, then he walked away.

I heard him leave the house a short while later.

Once I was satisfied with the number of gifts that I'd gotten so far, I made a few notes of the ideas I'd come up with that morning after picking the boys' brains a little bit. I made sure to tuck that note into my purse as I prepared to head out.

Through the front window, I could see that the day had dawned cold and frosty. I could still see streaks through the front yard where squirrels had scampered about, heading for their trees after scavenging for any acorns that might have fallen in the night. Birds trilled in the trees, the last few who had either decided to stay through the winter or who had yet to leave. My time in the city had me longing for their presence, and now that it would be some time before I heard their songs again, I found myself a little more somber than I had thought I would be.

I grabbed my coat from the coat rack in the front hall, along with my favorite hat and scarf. I could hardly believe how cold it had become so quickly. It was the same sort of chill we'd experienced as kids, living not much further south than this, still in the foothills of the mountains.

Whistling a tune, I gave a tug to the front door of the truck, to open it. The door caught, stuck tight.

I tried again, but it wouldn't budge.

I blinked, looking down the length of the vehicle. Had I been so lost in my thoughts that I forgot to unlock it? I hardly ever bothered to lock it in the first place. I lived with the sheriff of the town, after all. Anyone dumb enough to come and try to steal my truck would have another think coming.

It wasn't locked, I realized. The handle pulled like usual, but it seemed like it was being pulled from the other side, as if someone were inside lying flat on the seat, trying to prevent me from coming in. Obviously, there wasn't anyone on the inside, and I had no reason to think that anything had gone wrong since I drove it around town yesterday.

I glowered at it. "Don't like the cold, huh?" I asked as if the truck would be able to answer. "Don't worry, you're in good company with me."

My words must have eased the truck's worries, as I pulled the door open with hardly any further delay.

"Hmm," I said, smiling. "All you needed was a little buttering up, huh – "

"Ugh!"

I glanced up, and peering around the back of the cab, spotted a woman walking away from Mr. Thompson's front door. Her heels clacked angrily against the driveway, and she wobbled as she struggled to pull a white, furry glove over her bare hand.

Who is she? I wondered.

Hair as red as a campfire flame, cropped close to her chin, framed her thin face. She wore glasses with thick, black, round frames, and even from this distance, I could see the holly red of her lipstick. Surprisingly enough, she wore a nurse's uniform similar to the ones in the hospital in Liberty City, except hers had a longer skirt and a large, red cross on the pocket.

She let out a yelp, arms flailing before she managed to grasp onto the hood of her car; her unseasonable footwear had let her down when she stepped on what could only have been some slick frost.

Oh, dear.

She staggered around the outside of the car, holding tight to any part she could, before wrenching the door open and climbing inside. She wasted no time starting the ignition and backing out onto the street.

I watched the car disappear before turning and getting inside of my own vehicle.

A nurse showing up at the Thompson household. That was interesting, wasn't it?

Sliding the key into the ignition, I hesitated for a moment.

Well, a nurse could mean one of two things, couldn't it? It could be a good thing, because it would mean that Mr. Thompson could be getting treatment for whatever had been keeping him trapped inside forever. Maybe his son had had enough of waiting on him and decided to try and hire someone to help him. A house-visiting nurse made a lot of sense, then.

I started the truck and turned to watch over my shoulder as I backed out of the driveway.

Either that, or Mr. Thompson had taken a turn for the worse. It could be that his condition was becoming unmanageable, and more help was needed.

I shook my head. This wasn't any of my business, was it? I had no reason to sit here and consider their troubles, did I? Vicky and I had agreed on it. Craig and Roger had agreed on it with us.

The neighbors' troubles were their own. I certainly had enough on my own plate without adding worry about Mr. Thompson.

...But then why was that nurse so infuriated when she left the house?

There was little room for doubt about how the woman was feeling when she left. Exasperated was right up there with irate. I'd heard her exclamation as she was leaving.

Why was she leaving in such a huff? What had happened?

I could almost guess.

Mr. Thompson, being the lovely, caring, kind soul

that he always was, must have been the cause. Given what Craig had told me about him, he likely chased her out, refusing help even if he desperately needed it for the sake of his wounded pride. He must have said some pretty terrible things for her to leave the way she had.

What in the world is going on over at that house?

I gazed out the window at it as I drove by, trying to catch sight of anything – of *anyone* – that might be able to provide a clue. All the drapes had been drawn closed, and there wasn't a shred of Christmas decoration to be seen anywhere around the entirely of the property. If it weren't for our lights or the garland and decorated tree in the front yard of the neighbor on the other side, you never would have known that Christmas was only a week away.

Something awful must have been happening in that house, and it made my skin crawl to even look up at it like I was.

At least someone from the outside managed to find their way in, I mused as I turned off Pine Street and headed for Main. It was something that Vicky and I hadn't been able to do, nor Craig and Roger.

Somehow, though, it really didn't make me feel any better.

That would all have to wait, as I was getting nearer to my destination. My nerves all hummed in unison, urging me to turn around and just head home. I really didn't *need* to make this trip. I'd made the crazy decision to visit this person in the middle of the night the night before. I knew he'd probably be able to help me better than anyone else could...

All it would take was a visit from me.

How hard could that be?

Those thoughts were all well and good before I managed to fall back to sleep for several more hours, but in the light of day, it really didn't feel like it made a lot of sense.

Nevertheless, I'd committed to the idea and I was going to see it through...for Craig's sake.

I turned down a familiar dirt road, my truck bouncing along as I passed by fields that had been bedded down for the winter. A large, red tractor stood out in the midst of the sprawling soil, waiting for its turn again in a few months' time.

A charming farmhouse waited for me at the end of the drive, and to my relief, I saw a car parked there that I had really hoped to see. It would have angered me to no end if I had mustered up the courage to come all the way out here just to find out that he wasn't home in the first place.

"Oh, *hello*, Barbara!" said the sweet-faced woman at the door when I knocked. She beamed at me, waving me inside. "Come in, *come in*. What a pleasure it is to see you again."

"Hello, Miss Bonnie," I said, my face warming at the sight of her excitement, realizing that it was just because I was there. "I was wondering if – "

"He most certainly is, dear, you just let me go get him for you, all right? Just wait here." She scurried off toward the kitchen with more speed than I would have expected from a woman her age.

I sat down on one of the leather armchairs with a baby blue doily draped over the back, as round as one of the wheels on that tractor out front. I stared at the intricately woven decoration absently for a little while as I tried to will my heart to stop beating so erratically –

"Barbara?"

I jumped out of the chair like it had bitten me, and looked up to see Roger standing in the quaint, eclectic living room. "H – Hi," I said, trying to steady myself but instead getting my foot caught on the leg of the chair. I reached out to catch myself. "Sorry – sorry for bothering you at home like this, but there was something I wanted to talk to you about without Craig overhearing."

Roger's gaze hardened. "And what might that be?" he asked.

"It's nothing bad, don't worry – "

"Is this about that neighbor of yours?" he asked in a flat, cold tone.

"*Roger*," the older woman snapped, giving him a whack on the arm with the back of her hand. "You do *not* speak to a lady like that! Especially not a lady who – "

"I'm sorry, Miss Bonnie," he said obediently, then looked at me. "Sorry. Didn't mean to be so terse with you."

"It's all right," I said. "But no, that's not why I'm here."

His thick brows came together. "Then what is it?"

I swallowed hard, looking away. "I – I was hoping you might help me figure out what to get Craig for Christmas."

"Oh, how sweet..." Miss Bonnie murmured. "Now, you just take a seat again here, dear, and I'll get you all some hot coffee. Cream and sugar?"

"Yes, thank you," I said, not daring to lower myself back into the chair until I could see that he was going to help me.

To my shock, a smile had grown on Roger's face.

"What?" I snapped. Now it was my turn to be terse. "What's that look for?"

The smile widened, and he shook his head. "Coming to me for help, huh? Ran out of options?"

I glared at him, as the both of us took our respective seats. "In case you've forgotten, you're my brother's right hand man. It seemed obvious to come to you first."

Roger nodded. "Have you talked to the boys yet?" he asked.

"Not about ideas for their dad, no. Besides, I've heard them talking about a new football or a wrench set." I shook my head. "I wanted to get him something…more."

"How so?" he asked. "Craig would be happy with anything you would want to get for him."

"Yes, but this is our first Christmas together since we were kids," I said. "I thought about getting him something to make him laugh, but…I don't know, that just doesn't feel right."

"Why not?" he asked.

"Well…" I said, scratching the back of my neck, the blushing only getting worse. These things all made sense in my head, but now that I was saying them out loud, I really was starting to wonder why I felt the need to come down here in the first place. "I don't know. Bringing me into the picture was the biggest change in their family's life since Becky died.

I can't help but feel the desire to make the holidays... well, special."

Roger said nothing, just patiently sat with his hands knit together in front of himself, looking much older in that moment than he usually did. *And the way he's sitting there, all attentive and listening to me, he's much more attractive than he usually seems –*

I pushed that thought aside and cleared my throat. "I want to thank him somehow for letting me stay with them. It's been one of the best things to happen for me in a long while, and...well, I just want to make sure that I'm giving Craig something he deserves."

Roger nodded. "I can understand where you're coming from. But don't you think you're putting a little too much pressure on yourself?"

"How so?"

"You're expecting this Christmas to be perfect. You think that if you don't get him something out of this world that he'll be disappointed. And that's just not true. Besides, what about next year? You're going to feel obligated to try and top it somehow."

I hadn't thought of that.

"Craig never would have asked you to stay with him if he didn't want you to," Roger said.

"It's not that I'm worried he doesn't want me there,"

I said. "It's just…I imagine he must be missing his late wife an extra amount this year, and yet at the same time, I know he's pleased I'm there since I'm helping take care of the house and the boys and all that…"

He waited for me to finish my thought, but I didn't know how to.

"Have you come up with any ideas?" Roger asked. "Anything that's feasible, that is?"

"It's going to sound ridiculous…but the only things I can think of are things that he wanted as a kid, but never got," I said.

"Like what?" he asked.

"You know…toys, gadgets, things like that. We never really had the money for anything fancy or expensive, and my parents…well, they never would have paid that close attention to us all individually in the first place. There were five of us, of course, and because of that, we never really got very much."

Roger's expression softened ever so slightly. "Craig's mentioned your parents probably as many times as I have fingers on this hand," he said, waving them at me.

I looked away. "Can't say I'm surprised about that," I said. "So, I don't know, I must be nostalgic or something, thinking about all those things that he never could get as a kid. But why would he want those things now? He's a grown man. I should get him socks, or a tie, or something like that."

Roger shook his head, shrugging. "Well, why not get him those things that he wanted when he was a kid?"

I blinked at him. "That's...not what I expected you to say," I said.

He chuckled. "There's always a part of us that never really grows up, never grows out of those desires. Can't you think of anything that you wanted as a child that you never got?"

"A Sally Anne doll," I said, then froze.

I blushed.

He smirked.

"See? I thought so."

"That's – that's different, though," I said. "I can't imagine he'd actually want a toy or something like that."

"You'd be surprised," he said. "Besides, it's not often the gift that matters. It's the thought behind it. And what's more thoughtful than giving him something that only you could give. You were the only one there to hear any of those wishes when he was a kid. It should be you."

I contemplated it for a moment. Really, it wasn't a bad idea. In fact, it actually made a lot of sense.

"But how would I – I wouldn't even know where to look for these things."

"There's a great second-hand shop off Randolph that might have what you're looking for," Roger said. "Lots of great stuff. If not there, then there's Harold's toy place on Jefferson."

"Oh…" I said. "All right. I guess…I guess I'll try there."

"Here's the coffee, dears," said the cheery Miss Bonnie as she reentered the room, carrying two mugs filled with steaming coffee.

I stayed for a short while, making small talk with the both of them before I excused myself and headed out.

My heart pounded as I stole a glance through my rearview mirror. I thought I saw Roger standing there on the front porch, watching me go, but I didn't know if that was just my mind playing tricks on me.

I didn't like that I didn't really know how any of that made me feel. He'd been indignant, presumptuous, and also kind, thoughtful. He knew my brother well. I had been right to go to him. However, I didn't know what to think of the fact that he seemed to be getting to know me, too.

Craig must talk about me when they're together or something. He's probably trying to set me up with him.

I shook my head, gripping the steering wheel more tightly.

Roger Elwood was *not* the sort of man I'd ever want to be with. He was stodgy, derisive, rough around the edges. He found my frustration amusing, and treated me like a child even more than Craig did.

And yet I couldn't quite forget the softness of his gaze as I told him about what I had wanted to do for Craig. For once, he didn't ridicule me or tell me I was being stupid. Instead, he wholeheartedly encouraged me.

"Agh..." I groaned, turning onto the paved road and heading back toward town.

It seemed I had some thinking to do, and not a whole lot of time left to do it.

I stopped at the stop sign at the end of the street. I had a little bit of time before everyone came home for the day, and still had to stop at the grocery...

What's the harm? I thought, and turned right instead of left, heading toward Randolph.

Who knew what treasures I might find?

7

I really shouldn't have been surprised, but the grocery market was much, much busier than I was used to seeing it. I'd developed a comfortable routine where I'd go in every Tuesday morning. It seemed to be the best time when children were in school and most sensible mothers had their shopping done for the week the day before. The busyness of the weekend had yet to hit, and those wishing to restock their ice box had done so Monday when they had their first chance after it being closed on Sunday.

A group of ladies collecting money for the soup kitchen were selling big, beautiful poinsettias. They had every shade of red, pink, and white, which made me feel that much more festive as I walked through the front doors.

I'll get one on the way out.

I pulled my list from my purse, knowing that I only had about another half an hour before I had to be home to start the beef stew if I wanted it to be nice and tender to give to the boys and Craig at a reasonable hour. I'd hate to make them wait for me just because I decided to do a little bit of shopping today.

"Pardon me," I said as I accidentally elbowed a woman bending at the waist to peer at a shelf of canned yams. She squinted so hard that her top lip wrinkled.

"Can you read this for me?" she asked, snatching a can off the shelf and thrusting it into my hands. "What's in this?"

I turned the can over in my hand. "Yams," I said, offering it to her. "Are you looking for something else?"

She took the can and set it in the basket hooked in the crook of her arm. "No, I just wanted to make sure there weren't any spices in it. My husband can't stand those sweet yams, and neither can I. Thanks so much. You've saved me a headache."

She headed off with a wave.

I watched her go even as another woman tried to sidle past me in the narrow aisle.

"Excuse me," she said.

"That's quite all – " I began, catching sight of her cropped, red hair the same color as the yams in the cans sitting on the shelf right beside me.

I gasped. It was the nurse that was leaving Mr. Thompson's house earlier that afternoon!

"Miss?" I asked, reaching out to her.

She stood quite a few inches taller than I, but that could have been because of the sleek, black heels she wore. She turned to look at me, and I knew immediately that I was correct. Her slightly puckered lips were as red as some of those poinsettias outside, and her square-framed glasses were not black this close, but a deep, cobalt blue.

She blinked her icy blue eyes at me, her pencil brows furrowing. "Are you speaking to me?"

"Yes, I am," I said. "I'm sorry to bother you, but I believe I saw you leaving the house of my next door neighbor this afternoon."

The woman's eyes darted up like she was resisting the urge to roll them. "You are going to need to be a little more specific," she said. "I'm a visiting house nurse, after all. I have several patients that I see regularly." She had a rich, clear voice, and the intensity of her stare surprised me. She reminded me of one of the floor managers that I worked for back in Liberty City, who never laughed, and I hardly ever saw smile. She was not the sort of woman to cross, which was how this woman seemed as well.

"Mr. Thompson on Pine," I said. "I was just leaving my house when I saw you in his driveway, leaving too."

Eyes widening, she pursed those small lips of hers. "You saw me, did you? And I suppose you saw me nearly trip and fall on my face on that black ice?"

Oops. She thinks I'm making fun of her. "I'm sorry, I'm not trying to embarrass you or anything like that. Furthest thing from it."

She crossed her arms, rolling her shoulders a bit. "Yes, that was me. Why do you ask?"

"Were you there to visit old Mr. Thompson?" I asked.

She glanced down the aisle in both directions. "...Maybe it would be better if we were to step out of the way and talk?"

"Yes, of course," I said.

She turned and headed down to the end of the aisle, and I caught up to her just as she was walking back out of the store and into the crisp afternoon.

The sun had started to set, bathing the parking lot in golden hues. The nurse's hair, too, looked like tongues of flame, and as she tossed it out of her eyes, I might have believed it was truly alight.

She turned when we were standing well away from the front door, out of anyone's way – and out of earshot, too, I noticed – and crossed her arms. "Now, who are you, exactly? Did you follow me here? Did the doctor send you?"

"Doctor Ted? No, no," I said. "I'm Barbara Hollis. I live next door to Mr. Thompson. I'm Sheriff Hollis' sister."

The woman's eyes grew even wider behind her glasses. "The sheriff? I had no idea he – that he lived right – oh, goodness me…"

Now it was my turn to be concerned. "Why do you say it like that?"

"It's just – you're a complete stranger, why should I tell you anything?" she asked.

"Well, you certainly don't owe me anything, except I already gave you my name," I said, believing more and more with each passing minute that this woman might have a lot more value than I'd initially considered. A nurse gone to visit Mr. Thompson; how convenient.

But she was hiding something. I knew because

I'd been dealing with these sorts of people a lot lately. That, and *I* was hiding something. I recognized the signs, most notably that she brought me well away from everyone and everything. She didn't want anyone to overhear us. Not that I wanted that. I should have probably considered it as well when I struck up a conversation with her in the middle of the grocery aisle –

"My name...is Nancy Clemmons," she said finally, with concerted effort. "I'm sorry, this is all a bit strange. I've never had anyone recognize me out in public like this, especially not a complete stranger. You're new in town, aren't you?"

"I moved to Cobbsville a few months ago, yes," I said. "I'm living with my brother and his boys for the time being."

"I see..." she said. "And...you said you saw me leaving Mr. Thompson's this morning? Were you spying on me?"

"No," I said. "I just happened to hear you leave. If I'm honest, you sounded more than a little frustrated."

"Did you hear anything else?" she asked.

She wouldn't have asked that question if there wasn't more that could have been heard. Something important. "No, that's all I heard," I said. "And saw you leave." I tactfully left out the part where she slipped and nearly landed on her backside. That was what had embarrassed her in the first place.

She clicked her tongue, looking away. "Yet you recognized me here in the grocery store? When you saw me so briefly?"

What was with the twenty questions? *Now I know what other people must feel like when I've asked them about some of the other cases I've worked on...*

I'd need to be better about that going forward.

"You have distinct features," I said. "Most notably, your hair being even redder than mine. That, and your glasses."

She reached up and briefly touched the frames resting on her cheekbones. "I see," she said once more. "You must be quite perceptive. Either that, or you have an excellent memory. Hardly anyone I know would be quick to remember a face they had only seen once."

Hard to forget someone who was trying to ice skate in high heels this morning and failing miserably. "Let's just say that a certain level of insightfulness runs in the family," I said.

An appreciative smile stretched across her sharp face. "It must," she said. "Well, I'm assuming that this conversation has little to do with me and everything to do with Mr. Thompson. Is that correct?"

I began to wonder why this woman was a nurse and not a private detective or something. *Maybe I should make Craig aware that there's someone whose services might be valuable to the police...if she was interested, that is.* "That is correct," I said. "You said you were a nurse. I assume you were going to visit old Mr. Thompson and not his son?"

"That's precisely what I was trying to do," she said. "But I was turned away upon entry."

"Turned away?" I asked. "Why on earth would they turn away a nurse, especially if his health is failing like many of his neighbors are worrying is happening?"

"I have no idea," she said. "I still don't. I show up as scheduled today, and his son wouldn't even let me inside out of the cold for a moment."

My brow furrowed. "That's odd."

"That's what I thought," she said, folding her arms, her hands disappearing in the folds of her thick, wool parka. "That son of his fired me right there on the spot."

"What?" I asked in disbelief.

"I know, I know," she said. "I can hardly believe it."

"Why?" I wondered. "Wouldn't they have expected you to come?"

"You would certainly think so," she said. "I visit every two weeks. I hadn't been able to make it two weeks ago, but that was near Thanksgiving and I had gone traveling to see some family – that's not important. What is important is that I have been going to see Mr. Thompson for the better part of six months now, and they turn me away without any notice?" She shook her head.

This whole situation just seemed to get stranger and stranger, and all it did was make me all the more concerned about Mr. Thompson. "Do you have any idea what's happening with him?"

"No," she said. "And – I suppose I don't know how much I should share with you, because he's my patient and all."

"Could you tell me if there was anything about his health that might have been declining?" I asked. "Anything worrisome?"

"He is an old man," she said. "He had health troubles at every turn. But was there something significant? No. I can at least tell you that much."

"All right," I said. *Then the only explanation I have is that there is something personal going on between him and his son. Right?*

"Honestly...I hope that it's not because what I said got back to him."

Something she said? Why would she volunteer that information if she had no intention of sharing it? "What did you say?" I asked.

She looked around, shivering in a way that reminded me of a bird shaking off the rain. "I...probably shouldn't say this. I could lose my job if it got back to my bosses."

"Then why tell me at all?"

She screwed up her face, tapping her heel for a few seconds. "Because it's been bothering me all day, and I don't know you from Adam. I couldn't tell anyone that I really know. That wouldn't look good."

"So...you want to confess to me?" I asked.

"Why are you so interested in all of this?" she asked. "Are you and my patient friends?"

I wasn't sure how much I should share in this situation. Just as she had her confidentiality, so I had mine. On one hand, telling her that Mr. Thompson and I were friends might make her hesitant to repeat whatever she had said. It was clear that it had not been anything all that good, hence her concern about it getting back to him. On the other, she might find it a little strange that I hardly knew him and wanted to know so much about his life.

I knew which one seemed the most logical, and the most promising. "He's lived next to my brother for the entire time he's lived in Cobbsville, which has been for many years," I said. "I know my brother has been a little concerned. We haven't seen our neighbor out for his walks lately, or even going out to get the newspaper."

Her brow furrowed. "But your relationship..."

"If you're worried that I would be affronted by anything negative said about him, then you can relax," I said. "We know that he's ungrateful and difficult, and because of it, we know that he's done a good job of pushing people away."

She visibly relaxed, exhaling. "All right. Then I had the right read of you. Okay, I will tell you that when I said what I said, I was not having the best day already. I woke up to my dog throwing up all over the foot of my bed, and then slipped in the shower which wrenched a muscle in my back. I went to the office with a pack of ice that I pressed to my back every few minutes."

Was all this information necessary? Maybe not, but it was her way of justifying what happened. I would let her keep talking. When trying to get facts, one should never stop a witness from giving away free information.

"Anyway," she said after drawing in a fresh breath, her exhalation floating on the air. "I spent some time that morning over a cup of coffee venting my frustration to a coworker about the patient I needed to go see later that morning." She nodded, raising a hand, palm up with a shrug. "You know."

"I know which patient you mean," I said.

"Right. I was quite plain that day that I hated visiting him because of how – of how rude he is. All the time. From the moment I walked in the door, he would criticize everything I did, every recommendation I made for him. I was never there long, essentially long enough to get basic vitals – heart rate, breathing, blood pressure, you know – but he managed to get under my skin every time I sat there in his living room, trying to help him."

"You said you started going six months ago?" I asked.

"Yes," she said. "At the recommendation of his doctor. He reminded me regularly of this fact, mainly that he disagreed with Doctor Ted's decision, but the good doctor didn't want Mr. Thompson to have to drive back and forth once every two weeks."

"And so you complained a little about a difficult patient," I said. I shook my head. "There's no harm in that."

"That's…not all," she said. "I'm sorry, I just despise the fact that I said this out loud, because it might very well have been the reason why Mr. Thompson and his son wanted to let me go."

I was surprised that she wanted to tell me at all. Why would she have decided to when she was as worried as she was?

"…All right, I might as well say it. I may have been overheard saying that I couldn't wait for him to – to kick the bucket so that I wouldn't have to go over there anymore."

She frowned, her pointed features even sharper as she stared down at the ground. Her breath came quickly, her anxiety given away by the frequent puffs of warm air floating in front of her face.

So she had wanted him dead so that she wouldn't have to go back.

If Mr. Thompson had already died, then I would have definitely thrown her in with the list of suspects. However, her admission might have made me reconsider that eventually. Why would she have openly told me that? It had been for nothing more than to absolve herself of guilt for what she had said, which she clearly felt badly about.

Is it guilt? Or is she upset that she was overheard because it might have cost her one of her patients?

"It sounds – *awful* – and I know that. I never should have said it. As a nurse, especially. I was just – frustrated, and if you had to try and take care of him when he clearly had absolutely no interest in being cared for, then you would want to pull your hair out, too."

"I can believe it," I said. "He is insufferable on the best of days."

"Thank you," she said, but there wasn't much feeling in it. She surveyed the parking lot, squinting against the dying light. "But I never meant – of course I want the best for my patients, no matter how hard they might be to deal with."

"But you still think that what you said got back to them somehow? And that's why his son turned you away?"

"I don't know, honestly, but that's all I can think," she said. "Like I said, I hadn't visited very recently, but the last time I was there, everything was fine. Well, as fine as it usually is. This time, though, Gerald was short with me, saying they no longer needed me, and wouldn't even give me a chance to explain myself."

I frowned. That did seem strange. "How long has Mr. Thompson's son been there with him?" I asked. "Maybe he's taken up some of the responsibility of caring for his father? He's certainly taken over his father's daily tasks like getting the mail, taking the trash out, those sorts of things."

She shook her head, laughing. "Gerald? No. He's lazy. He never did anything when I was there. Sat on the sofa, watching television."

"Really?" I asked.

She nodded. "He moved in earlier this year, but I've only spoken to him a few times. He usually stays out of the way during my visits, but I walked in more than once to hear them fighting with each other."

"About what?"

"Anything," she said. "The worst one was when some milk had spoiled at the back of the refrigerator, and Mr. Thompson made it seem like his son did this on the regular. He only cared about himself, never going out of his way to help others."

Then why was he caring for his father in the ways I've seen?

Something was not adding up. Whatever was going on in that house, neither Gerald nor his father wanted people to see.

"And you couldn't tell me there was anything obviously wrong with Mr. Thompson's health?" I asked.

"It was steadily declining," she said. "Like I said, that's why I was brought on in the first place."

"I heard he requested that some of his medicine be stopped, too," I said.

Her brow furrowed. "Which one?"

"Nothing detrimental, but something for his joint pain," I said.

She shook her head. "That man – he is so stubborn sometimes, it drives me crazy. He fought me about that one for so long, since it's not exactly necessary, in his opinion, and expensive. In reality, it's not *that* pricey, not as pricey as some of the others that I helped him find more affordable options for. Doctor Ted wanted him to use those specific pain relievers because he knew it would help him sleep, and without sleep, he'd be more apt to sickness in general."

"So he thinks that because he's fired you, that he can just drop whatever medicine he wants?" I asked. "Doesn't he realize that it might make his life overall more difficult, not having you and these medicines?"

"That's exactly what will happen," she said. "I'll have to ask Doctor Ted if he's going to send a different nurse there to take care of him. He needs it. He cannot take care of himself, and that son of his is as good as useless. He might as well expect one of the armchairs to take care of him. It might do a better job."

"That does surprise me that he'd be so useless..." I said. "Why would he want to have his son come live with him if they were going to fight all the time and he wasn't going to help him?"

"Maybe he was all he had..." she answered.

I sighed, shaking my head. "I guess I just wish I knew how he was doing," I said. "There are a lot of people who are concerned about him. We hate to think the worst, but – "

"I might not be a great deal of help, but there could be some who would be able to tell you more," she said. "Down at Anderson Park, there are a group of men who get together every week and play chess. Mr. Thompson frequented those games, as I think it was one of his only social outings of the week."

My eyes widened. "That could be useful," I said. "Maybe one of those men would be able to get us up to speed." *Or maybe give us an insight into Mr. Thompson's life so that if we needed a reason to go kick in the door, we'd be able to.* "Do you have any idea when he would go down there?"

"Every Monday, I believe," she said. "Though I wonder if they're meeting, since it's the week before Christmas."

"I'm guessing the group is made of mostly older men? Many of them live for that time together at the park."

She nodded. "You're right."

"Well, thank you. I appreciate you being willing to talk to me about all this."

"You're welcome, I guess. And if you could be so kind as to not repeat what I said – "

I raised a hand. "Don't worry, I won't say a word."

"Thank you," she said. "Though if I'm honest, I am not going to be terribly unhappy to say goodbye to that family and all their trouble."

"You have no idea how much I understand that sentiment," I said. "One can only hope that they eventually see that their troubles affect the people around them."

She didn't look convinced. Neither was I.

"It was nice to meet you," I said, holding my hand out to her.

She took it, shaking it. "And you, Miss Hollis. Please tell your brother I think he does a wonderful job taking care of our town."

"I'll pass on the message," I said. "And I hope that you manage to find a family that appreciates your services more than Mr. Thompson did."

"You're sweet," she said. "I should get going. Have a good day."

"You, too."

She headed across the parking lot, drawing her collar up around her neck, the ends of her bright hair bouncing in time with her steps.

Firing a nurse. Refusing medicines from the doctor.

This seemed more and more suspicious with each passing moment…and I just couldn't figure out how far down the rabbit hole we were going.

How bad were things getting? Was it all just a huge misunderstanding?

It was difficult to say. I'd need to go down to the park and speak with those men.

8

There was nothing I could do to make Monday come any faster, and so I decided to try and distract myself as best I could.

All I could do was hope that nothing serious happened next door before I had the chance to meet with some of Mr. Thompson's friends. I hoped against all hope that they would be able to give me good information, information that I could then take to Craig.

Something had to be done, I was almost positive... I just didn't know what we might be up against.

The boys were home, and since it was only four days until Christmas, we decided to turn up the radio and listen to Christmas music all day until we heard every song repeated at least twice.

"Hey, Tim? Where'd we put the ribbons?"

"In here, Aunt Barb!" he called.

I stepped out of the kitchen and into the living room, padding past Toby who lay flat on his stomach in front of the television again, watching TV.

I found Tim sitting at the table, gift wrap spread all over the table, with bits of ribbon scattered around and some bows, many of which looked like practice, thrown around.

"Don't look!" he cried, throwing his hands over whatever he was in the middle of wrapping.

"Sorry," I said with a laugh, shielding my eyes. "I figured you knew I was coming!"

"No," he said, reaching across the table, hands closing around a spool of ribbon. He thrust it toward me. "Here. Take it."

"Thank you," I said with a laugh, taking it.

"I don't have a lot of time," Tim said. "Dad will be home in a little while. I have to finish wrapping your gifts and then his, and I don't know if I'll be able to get it all done!"

"I can help you wrap Craig's," I said.

Tim looked up, considering. "All right. If I have underestimated the time, then I'll let you know."

I grinned. This kid's determined faces were really starting to grow on me.

"Great," I said. "Just come get me. I'm getting the last few things wrapped up for you, too."

His jaw dropped. "When I'm *home*?" he exclaimed.

Laughing, I turned away. "You've been home for the last three days," I said over my shoulder. "When am I supposed to find the time? See, I'm in the same predicament that you are. Just don't come into the kitchen without telling me first."

His face scrunched up, and for a brief second I knew I had caught sight of what he must have been like as a three-year old. A bubble of guilt rose and popped at the thought; *I can't change the past. All I can do is do my best to enjoy the relationship I'm building with them now.*

I headed back through the living room, and my eyes fell on Toby again. As I walked by, I took a peek at his face. He was watching one of his favorite movies, yet his eyes were cast down toward the carpet, his head tilted to the side, cradled in his hands.

Pausing, I waited until he felt my gaze on his face.

His eyes cleared, whatever deep thought he had

been lost in fading. He blinked, then smiled, lowering his hands. "Hey, Aunt Barbara. What's going on?"

I took a seat on the arm of the sofa. "I'm just getting the last few of my Christmas presents wrapped," I said, glancing toward the tree set up in the corner beside the fireplace behind him. "It's looking pretty full under there. I take it you finished wrapping yours?"

He shook his head, turning his gaze back to the television.

"Well, what are you waiting for?" I asked.

He shrugged.

"I'd be happy to help you," I said. "I picked up some really nice paper the other day, and I could teach you a really easy way to wrap the presents – "

"I know how to wrap them," he said.

All right, then.

"Is everything okay?" I asked. "You don't seem as excited about everything as you did earlier."

"I'm fine," he said automatically, still not looking at me. His gaze might have been fixed on the television, but it had grown distant.

I hesitated. I didn't know where the boundary might be for him. I wasn't his mother, and definitely didn't want to seem like I was trying to be. On the other hand, I did live with the two of them and their dad. Wasn't it partially my responsibility to help take care of them? Did that not include when something was bothering them?

"That means you aren't fine," I said, folding my arms. "I was your age once. I know that's difficult to believe, but I know exactly what that means. It's been that way since the dawn of time, kid. What's eating you?"

He didn't look at me for a few seconds, but then those eyes that looked so much like his dad's flicked up to meet my own. He rolled onto his side and sat up, propping himself up on his arm. "I'm just worried that Dad won't even be here to open gifts. So...why bother?"

And the truth comes out. My heart sank. Of course this had to do with Craig.

Toby always acted like the strong one. He always pretended like he didn't need Craig, but I could see the hurt in his eyes when we would sit at dinner together and Craig would get an urgent call that he needed to take right then and there. Toby would brush it off, making some sort of joke, but I was starting to see that this affected him just as much as it did his brother; his brother just wore his heart on his sleeve.

I knew I needed to approach this cautiously. I could do more harm than good if I were too supportive *or* too dismissive. "I take it this has happened before?" I asked. I already knew the answer, but I thought it might give him a chance to blow off some steam.

He nodded, tracing the tip of his finger through some of the frays in the rug. "Last year he was gone all day. We didn't even get dinner that night. If it weren't for the Fosters, we would have been all alone that day."

"I see," I said. "I'm sure that Christmas day can be both good and bad for a lot of families. Emergencies still happen, don't they?" *It doesn't really matter how we feel about it.*

"Why do they always seem to happen the one day that we just want Dad home?" he asked. "Every year, it seems like something comes up. He almost always misses Christmas Eve with us, and can't make it to dinner or the Christmas Eve service at the church. We usually go with the Fosters since they have us over every year beforehand for ham and mashed potatoes. Then on Christmas Day, he gets a call first thing in the morning that he has to deal with." Anger wrinkled his forehead. "I just wish that everyone would leave Dad alone! Is that too much to ask?"

"No, it's not," I said. "It's perfectly fine that you want your dad home with you on Christmas day. You want a day that you can have him all to yourselves. And everyone would understand that. I suppose this is just one of those hard lessons in life that not everyone is as benevolent as we wish they would be. Some people are selfish, and some people do stupid things. They ruin things for everyone else."

"Why, though?" Toby asked. "Why can't they think of anyone but themselves?"

"That's a good question," I said. "But those are the kinds of people who don't seem to realize that their actions affect others. Maybe they do and they don't care. Regardless, it's a reality that we have to face."

Toby frowned. "But why on Christmas day?"

"Because that's the day that matters most to you," I said, then shook my head. "No, that's not exactly it. It's because you want that day to be as perfect as it can be. Your dad gets calls every day, some even lasting well into the night. I know, I've been here long enough to see them. I've helped on some of those calls. But Christmas is the one day out of the year that he *should* be home. Everyone else gets to spend that day with their whole family, opening gifts, making memories together." I sighed. "And you and your brother sometimes have to make a sacrifice that you shouldn't have to by letting your dad go and help other people out."

Toby's brow furrowed together. "A sacrifice?"

I nodded. "That's what you guys are doing. You both are making an enormous sacrifice, one that you shouldn't have to. One that your dad hates that you have to make. But you know what? It takes a lot of bravery to be able to do what you both do."

Toby looked away. "I don't know…"

"I'm serious," I said.

He shook his head. "I'm the one being selfish by wanting him home, aren't I?"

I knelt down beside him. "No, Toby. Not at all. In fact, that's quite a mature observation. You're growing up. You feel like you shouldn't want that, but you aren't asking as much as you think you are. The world we live in may not be fair all the time, but you aren't being selfish by wanting your dad home with you."

He exhaled sharply, his nostrils flaring. "This is

such a small town. How can there be so many things wrong in it all the time?"

I smirked at him, sitting down and crossing my legs beneath me. "Things like this happen everywhere. People are people, you know? The good and the bad. Most people do good. Some, though...well, that's why we need people like your dad around."

"I know..." Toby said.

I studied him, watching his gaze sweep over the carpet. The wrinkles in his forehead told more than his words did; he really wasn't a little boy anymore. The child inside him was fighting with the man that was beginning to develop.

My heart stirred within me as I watched the struggle in him.

At twelve, he was facing difficult aspects of life that some people never did. He was learning the act of selflessness, and putting others before himself.

In that moment, I found myself fiercely proud of him and the man he would someday be. He had a long way to go, but Craig was doing right by his boys if they were not cowering from chances to grow.

I laid a hand on his shoulder. "Hey, I will do whatever I can to make sure that your dad is home for you on Christmas this year."

He looked up, confusion written on his face. "But how? What can you do?"

I smiled at him. "Well, I might not do what your dad wants, but sometimes even he needs help."

Toby's eyes brightened.

"Now, this might look like I'm going against what I just told you," I said. "Your dad asked me to stay out of the things he was dealing with. And he's right; those things aren't safe. I am not advocating for ignoring your dad. In fact, don't even think about it. However…I am in a unique predicament where I can help him despite the fact that I think he's being stubborn."

Toby smirked up at me. "Oh, that's for sure. You've done so much to help him; we've heard him say as much."

"Right," I said. "Not to brag or anything, but some of the cases he has worked on wouldn't have been solved if I wasn't helping him. He just needs more help. He and Elwood need more hands to help them figure everything else out – " I stopped. "I'm sorry. Your dad knows what he needs. He knows he needs help, and I am doing my best to try and convince him that I could be that help."

"He's just worried about you getting hurt again," Toby said.

I looked at him. I hadn't even considered what he and his brother might have thought about me getting involved with these murder investigations. Of course they would have noticed everything that would have happened, including the times when I'd come back home beat up.

What had they thought of that?

That comment was more of a reflection of how he felt, and likely how Tim felt, about it.

They're all worried I'm going to get hurt again.

I chewed the inside of my lip. They might understand why I wanted to help Craig, but the implications of doing it...were they worth it? Did the good outweigh the hurt it might cause the boys?

This is what Craig was trying to stress, and I just wasn't seeing it.

I had a lot to think about.

Regardless, the immediate problem was still staring me in the face. The trouble with the Thompsons next door was sure to go south before long, and I did not want it to happen on Christmas day when stresses would certainly be at an all-time high. That might be the most likely day for something to happen.

As such, I now had greater motivation to help Craig figure this all out so the boys could have their dad, without interruption, for the entirety of the day. They should be able to look forward to Christmas day just like every other kid did.

I knew I couldn't anticipate every trouble that Craig would ever have to deal with or the town as a whole would ever see, but I could make sure that this particular one was resolved before Christmas Day.

At least…I hoped I'd be able to.

"I know your dad is worried about me," I said. "And I completely understand it. I've gotten myself into some pretty sticky situations, and because of that, I've realized that I…am not invincible."

Toby frowned.

I smiled reassuringly at him. "Hey, I know that now. I am not going to be so reckless. I have things that are too important to me to risk losing, yeah?"

Begrudgingly, it seemed, he returned my smile.

I reached out, ruffling his hair. "Come on. I think those gingerbreads are cool enough by now. We should get to decorating, otherwise we'll be here all night."

"Hey, Tim!" Toby called, bouncing to his feet to follow after me. "Decorating time!"

"Okay!" his twin answered. "Be there in a minute! Just have to – ow – finish this!"

I'd done and said the right thing. I was certain of it. Now, all I had to do was do my best to make good on my promise to him.

Otherwise...he might resent me as much as everyone else if his dad is called away on Christmas day.

9

Monday, I was starting to realize, might have been a bit of a saving grace. I'd hated the idea of waiting so long, but when Craig came home from the station with a list of things left to do for the community Christmas party, I knew that we had our work cut out for us.

"Not too bad."

These were the words of Deputy Elwood when he stood beside me at the punch bowl the night of the party, nodding approvingly as he looked around.

I smirked, taking a sip of the frothy, fruity drink that had once been my grandmother's recipe. She had always insisted on using lime sorbet when she started making it, and that was what we used. That, and a good strawberry soda – homemade, of course. The guys down at the soda fountain were kind enough to donate some so we could use it.

It was pretty good, all things considered. For only having a few days' notice, Craig, Elwood and I had managed to throw together a pretty decent party.

I held out my cup, gesturing toward the back near the windows. "I'm still impressed by your decorating skills, let alone the tree you chose."

To my astonishment, he smiled. "Thank you," he said, lifting his own glass. "Bob down at the tree farm told me that he hadn't been able to sell it to anyone else, being tall as it is."

The top branches just barely brushed against the ceiling. There'd been no room for a star.

"I appreciate your creative use of tinsel to tie the star around the top of the tree," I said. "And all the different colored lights give it a festive feel. The kids all seem to love it."

He shrugged, taking a sip of his drink. "Hard to be picky when it's all we had in the back from a couple of years ago. Most of the bulbs didn't work, so I needed to make three trips to the hardware store."

"Good use of your time," I said.

Families mingled about the space, at the cookie

decorating table, near the Christmas tree to select a gift donated by the church for the children. The back doors near the garage had been thrown open wide, letting the cool December air in. A smoker had been brought down from a nearby farm, and thick chops, steaks, and husked corn were all being cooked up for the guests.

"It looks like the whole town showed up," I said.

"'Course they did," he said, brow wrinkling as he looked down at me. "That's what always happens at parties. Oh, right. I forget that you're from the city. Never seen people come together like this, huh?"

"It's not that…" I said, my cheeks flushing pink. I crossed my arms. "We never really went to these sorts of things when we were kids, that's all."

Elwood studied my profile; I could feel his gaze on my hot face. "Craig's said as much," he said, but left it at that.

What has Craig told him about our difficult childhood?

"Don't look now, but Tim's following after that girl again," he said.

I followed his gaze, spotting the petite form of Elaine Foster and some of her friends heading outside toward the crowds gathered around the food. Tim followed after. I smirked.

"He's got it bad, huh?" Elwood said.

"Puppy love," I said. "They've been friends for a long time, and she gives him attention. Though I won't lie...I'd be happy if Tim had that sort of perfect love story to tell his kids one day."

Elwood snorted. "You really believe in that kind of stuff?"

"I do," I said, glaring up at him.

He chuckled. "Of course you do. I hate to break it to you, but love ain't all that mushy stuff you find in books."

"I am fully aware," I said, the color in my face growing redder.

He continued to chuckle.

"So how's that neighbor of yours behaving?" he asked. "Seen him wander out into the wide, open world yet?"

My heart skipped, the frustration I felt bursting like a pricked balloon. I stared up at him. "I – well, no. I haven't seen him yet."

His smile slipped. "Really?" he asked, his tone changing as quickly as my own had. "You haven't seen him at all?"

I shook my head. The party suddenly seemed too loud, and conversely far away at the same time. "Not yet, no."

He shifted his feet. "Still think something's wrong over there?"

"I do, yes," I said. "But why are you asking?"

His left brow arched. "I'm not stupid, you know. I know that you can't stop once you get started on these things."

"Did Craig say something?" I asked.

"Nope," Elwood said, shaking his head, his gaze sweeping the room. I recognized the same sort of behavior in Craig since moving in with him; it didn't matter where we were, he always looked alert, paying attention to everyone and everything around him. "He's been too focused on the party and getting everything ready for Christmas."

I swallowed hard, the punch settling like sour milk in my stomach. I set the glass down behind me on the bright red tablecloth. "What makes you think that I'm still worried about it?"

He took a look down at me, raising his brow again. "Are you?"

I couldn't keep eye contact.

"Exactly," he said, lowering his voice, leaning toward me. "Craig's likely forgotten about it. Let's keep it that way. No need to drag him into this again."

I turned my face up to him. This close, I noticed little flecks of gold in his eyes. "Are you saying that you'll help me?"

"I'm saying that I'd like to hear what's gotten you so stuck on this still," he said. "What have you seen?"

"Well...I might not have seen old Mr. Thompson, but I did see a home nurse leaving the house a few days ago," I said. "She looked furious, to say the least. I found out why."

"You went over and stuck your nose in it, didn't you?" he asked.

"I most certainly did not," I said, folding my arms and glaring. "Not this time, anyway. I actually ran into her at the grocer's completely by accident. I recognized her from her bright red hair and the glasses she wore. They stood out."

He rolled his eyes. "Only a woman would notice something like that."

"You should be thankful that I care about these things like I do," I hissed under my breath. "Because what she told me is part of the reason I'm still worried about what's happening next door."

I gave him a quick run down of what the nurse had shared with me, and he listened more intently than I had thought he might. He certainly kept an eye on his surroundings, but more than anything he nodded and glanced at me when I made a point.

"So she didn't get to see him either, then," Elwood said. "Not even a glance inside?"

"Not from what she told me, no," I said. I shook my head. "Maybe I'm crazy, but I keep wondering if she could be in cahoots with the son for some reason – "

He shook his head. "Nah. I doubt it. She willingly told you that she'd been overheard saying that she didn't like his father. That's harmless enough, and with the job she has, she'll have no trouble finding more patients to care for. If she really had something to do with Mr. Thompson falling ill, first I imagine Gerald wouldn't have turned her away that day, but more than that, she wouldn't have told you about the chess meetings in the park every Monday. That would lead you to snoop around some more, and if she had something like money to gain from all this, she would want to steer you away, not help you dig more."

"I suppose you're right," I said, frowning. "Though I couldn't help but wonder if maybe she'd been giving him some sort of drug to sedate him or something, make him more tolerable to work with when she was there, *and* keep her coming back."

He shrugged. "Honestly, that's not a bad theory. I just think that her interaction with his son would have gone differently, and she wouldn't have been so open with you about everything."

I nodded. It made enough sense.

"I do think it will be worth following up with what she said about the chess games in the park on Mondays," he said. "People there are sure to know him better than she ever did."

I blinked, glancing up at him. "Are you telling me I should go?"

He gave me a sidelong look, bobbing his head once, almost without my noticing.

"All right, then," I said. "Craig wouldn't be happy if he found out what I was doing."

"No, he wouldn't, which is why we need to keep this between us."

A young family stepped up to the table, with three children that were probably under the age of five. Roger and I stepped away, giving them space.

"Help yourself," I said, smiling at the kids. "It's my grandmother's special Christmas punch."

The oldest boy beamed at me, taking his younger brother's hand and holding it tight as their father filled a few glasses for them.

I smiled, and then glanced at Roger. His expression had become rather stern.

"What's the matter?" I asked.

He looked at me. "I just want to make sure that this town stays safe for people like them. They deserve it."

My teasing washed away like soap suds in a bath. "They certainly do."

We watched them make their way toward the door outside, the youngest child yawning wide in his mama's arms.

"You know, seeing that family with their kids… and thinking about families in general…" I said. "It makes me hope that something terrible hasn't happened between Mr. Thompson and his son."

"What are you most afraid of happening?" Roger asked.

My mouth fell open for a second, but my brain froze in mid-thought. I thought it would have been obvious, but I realized quickly that wasn't why he was asking me.

To think what I did was one thing…to say it out loud was another all together. If I really believed it, if I really thought it could be a possibility, then it would only strengthen my resolve. If not, then I'd realize pretty quickly how ridiculous I was being.

I cleared my throat. "I'm worried that Gerald's done something to his father...harmed him in some way." I looked up at Roger. "Maybe even the worst possibility."

He eyed me carefully. "You ever think you're just jumping at shadows?"

"All the time," I said. "But this feels different."

He sighed, crossing his arms. "I know Craig's explained this, but we can't go by your feeling alone. Even though the nurse couldn't get in and see him, that doesn't mean something's wrong. Families have a right to their privacy. They owe her nothing as a caretaker."

"I know that," I said, growing a bit petulant.

"You have to consider this from all sides, Barbara. We have nothing concrete to go on, apart from the fact that you haven't seen him in a couple of weeks. What if he broke his foot and can't walk? What if he's just much more sensitive to the cold than he used to be, and it makes all his bones and joints ache?"

My face grew hot, and I looked away. I might as well have been a scolded child.

"There are a lot of other possibilities at play here, things that honestly would be a lot more believable than thinking that Gerald's done something to hurt his father."

"But the nurse said they fought all the time – "

"Even if that's true, are you going to take her word for it?" he asked. "You met her once. You just want to believe what she said because it matches up with your own assessment. It fits your story."

I glowered at him.

He shrugged. "I'm sorry, but it's true. It's not always the worst case scenario. It's something you learn after doing what I do for as long as I have."

I didn't want to tell him that Craig had said something similar.

"That being said..." he went on, a bit quieter now. "I'm not too proud to realize that you have worked through these sorts of situations yourself before, especially recently. Not only that, but your instincts are good. You have an eye for stuff going wrong...and a way of just happening to be at the wrong place at the wrong time."

I shrugged. "It's a gift."

"For the record, I am not saying that I don't believe you," he said. "In fact, I do find it a bit odd that you haven't seen hide nor hair of Mr. Thompson. Craig's mentioned his surly nature before, how he chases the boys off his lawn when they kick balls over the fence and whatnot. Thing is, like I said, we can't go on your feeling alone."

"But why not?" I asked. "Either of those men could be hurt in there, and you won't go in because you don't have enough proof?"

"Think about what would happen if we did go break the door down, and we were wrong," he said. "We could get into a lot of trouble, possibly sued, not to mention losing the respect of a lot of people in town. We'd need some reasonable proof before we'd be able to look around."

I sighed, resisting the urge to snarl as an elderly couple passed by, greeting us with small waves.

We returned them, but I knew my smile must have looked anything but genuine.

Great, these people probably think we're having a lover's tiff or something –

"Fine. So I go on Monday. What is something I need to find out that *could* work as proof?"

"We may need to do some digging around the issue first," he said.

I groaned. "Roger, we don't have time! – "

"We don't have a choice," he said. "Sometimes, these matters have to be handled delicately, especially when someone from the outside isn't the one bringing you in."

"Yes, but I *am* bringing you in."

"You don't count," he said, shaking his head. "Not in the same way."

I exhaled, exasperated.

"Go see what you can find out," he said. "I'll give you full permission as the sister of the sheriff to ask any sort of questions you like, within reason, of course. Be kind to those old men; who knows if they have anything else to look forward to all week besides those chess games."

"Of course I will," I said.

A little time passed as we watched the party goers. Craig tramped into the room wearing a bright red Santa hat, carrying large bags beneath each arm.

"Must be time for one of Craig's games," I said.

Roger sighed. "Must be."

"Oh, come on, Roger. No desire to play along with my brother's goofy antics?"

His face slipped into a smile again as I gave him a shove in his elbow with my arm.

"We should have dressed you as Santa," I said. "Given you a red suit with big boots."

His smile grew. "No, I'd be terrible. I wouldn't know what to say."

"We could dye your hair white," I said. "Or rather

just sprinkle it with flour. With that beard of yours, it'd be completely believable."

He chuckled. "Maybe. Maybe I could do that next year."

I smiled, too. "You don't seem to hate the idea. I thought you really would."

He glanced at me. "Why's that?"

"Because it seems like you hate fun on principle."

He threw back his head and laughed at that, which might have been the first time I'd ever really seen it. He had a deep, belly laugh, and it sounded pleasant.

"See? You'd be great as Santa if you laughed like that a little more often," I said.

His laughter slowed, and he gave me a genuine, warm smile that spread all the way to his eyes. "You're not quite as insufferable as I originally thought you were, Miss Barbara."

"Hey," I said, some of the warm and fuzzy feelings fading. "You don't have to be a jerk."

"To you? Nah...maybe I don't need to be," he said.

"Good," I said, nodding firmly. "Then I'll make sure to tell Craig that you've volunteered to be Santa next year."

He shot me another grin, then chuckled.

It wasn't until Craig and I were on our way home that evening that it really occurred to me.

Had Roger Elwood and I actually agreed on something and gotten along? And did we really *laugh* together?

The world seemed to be coming undone at the seams, and I didn't know what to think of it.

10

Monday morning dawned bright and cold. I'd grown up in Georgia, and so a bitterly cold Christmas was not altogether rare, but it certainly had seemed to have eluded me during my time in Liberty City. *Must be due to the fact I lived so close to the ocean.*

There were no rumors of snow yet from the weathermen, but the twins simply could not help themselves whenever the weather report came through on the radio at the top of the hour.

"Oh, *please,* please let there be snow on Christmas day!" Tim exclaimed, crossing his fingers on both of his hands.

"Are we even far enough up in the mountains to

get snow?" I asked, sliding a shepherd's pie into the oven for dinner that night.

"Yeah!" Toby said from his place at the kitchen table; since our little chat, he'd been more willing to offer his help to me, especially in the kitchen. He swept some onion skins into a bowl to toss out into the compost pile in the backyard. "Three years ago, I think it was. No, four! We had a little bit, enough for us to make snowballs and throw them at each other for a little while!"

"It was great!" Tim said. "We had way more snow when Dad took us to Virginia a few years ago to go see one of his cousins. We even built snowmen!"

Toby gasped, looking at his brother. "What if it snowed that much *here?*"

Their volume continued to increase as they took off back toward their room.

Craig stepped into the kitchen, carrying an empty mug.

"They seem excited," he said.

"I thought I heard mention of going through their closets to find their snow clothes," I said with a chuckle.

I turned to look at him, and snorted.

"What?" he asked, smiling without knowing why.

"That turtleneck," I said with another snort. "I just can't take you seriously in it."

He looked down and gave the front of the maroon sweater a tug. "What's the matter with it?" he asked, chuckling with a disbelieving tone. "I thought it looked nice. Besides, it's warm."

"You look like our Papa," I said, dusting my hands off on my apron before untying it.

He smirked. "What, you mean this isn't the sort of fashion that would impress a lady?"

I stood on my tiptoes and pecked a kiss on his cheek. "Not this lady, anyway," I said.

"Where are you headed?" he asked, swinging around to follow me back out into the living room.

"Doing some last minute shopping," I said, lifting my coat off the coat rack.

He gawked at me. "Barb, it's two days until Christmas."

"I know," I responded placidly, tugging it on. I wondered if I'd dressed warmly enough. "Should I grab my scarf? Oh, I've got one in the truck."

Craig shook his head. "You must be crazy. It's going to be mayhem out there at the stores."

"I realize that," I said, pulling gloves out from my pockets, sliding them on. "Now, please take that pie out of the oven in an hour when the timer goes off.

I'm telling you so that you won't wonder what it's for when you hear it. Be ready for it, or you won't be having anything to eat for dinner tonight."

"Yes, Mother," he said with a smirk, striding toward his chair in the corner. He sank down into it. "Have a good time. Hope you find what you're looking for."

I hope so, too. "Bye!" I said with a cheery wave.

It wasn't *entirely* a lie. I did feel like I needed to pick up one more gift this year, something I'd debated for the last few nights. It didn't have to be anything special, I knew, because why should it be? It was nothing more than a nice gesture. And that was even if I'd have the chance to deliver it.

That's not important right now. First, you need to get down to the park and see what's going on there.

Right.

I'd been to the downtown park with the boys on a handful of occasions, mostly so they could play football with some of their friends when the weather was milder. It took up a huge corner of the town, surrounded entirely by big, old trees. It must have been there since the town's inception, given the fact that much of the town had been built around it and the church across the street. It had a soccer field, a baseball diamond, and some large patches of open green space for kids to play and dogs to run.

Even on such a chill day, people flocked there for a chance to breathe in the fresh air. Cobbsville was in no way like Liberty City, which was starved for real stretches of grass and trees that weren't installed by the hands of mankind. I had once thought it was a luxury to have a balcony of my own that overlooked one of those sparse stretches of earth that called itself a park. Here, in Cobbsville, I could really *breathe.*

And it suited me.

I had never really taken the time to look at everything the park had to offer. Bicyclists rode along the packed, dirt pathways. A man sat at an easel, painting the silhouette of the church steeple over the tops of the trees. A couple sat on a bench together, a wagon before them with a pair of young children, everyone eating a sandwich or sipping juice.

It wasn't as if I hadn't understood before, but walking amongst the townsfolk, yet feeling somehow separate from them with my mission, I realized that *this* was the reason why Craig and Roger did what they did. I'd had a taste of it myself before, but seeing people going about their days, entirely oblivious to my intentions, both chilled and humbled me. Chilled because what if I planned to strike someone out in the open, in the light of day? The chaos that would cause would be irreparable, especially to such little eyes and hearts. It humbled me…because it was the same thing I fought for. A safe and better tomorrow.

If there was something devious and wicked happening next door to my own house, then it needed to be stopped, for that kind of evil would not sit idly by. Soon, it would fester out into the rest of the world, poisoning it, too.

I breathed out, a puff of air hanging in front of me before I stepped right through it, like a train through its own engine smoke.

These thoughts were too deep for such a beautiful day.

Just as I was beginning to doubt the information that Nancy Clemmons had given me about a chess club meeting here, I spotted a group gathered at the far north-eastern corner of the park. Partially hidden by a weeping willow, I might have walked by it had it not been for a gentleman's raucous laughter that had drawn my attention.

Swiveling around, hands jammed tightly into the pockets of my jacket, I headed toward them.

It wasn't until I passed through what looked to

be the remains of a low, stone wall that I saw the dozen or so chess tables around the small clearing. They were surely permanent fixtures, made of heavy stone and marble tiles. Those nearest to me looked as if they had seen some love and wear over the years. Corners of the tiles chipped, cracks running through, some missing all together. Still, almost every table was occupied, and everyone there was an elderly man. All but one person: me.

"You're looking a little lost, dear," said a gentleman with sun-worn skin at the table to my right. He smiled at me, wrinkles appearing all up and down his face, not unlike a bulldog. "Come on in, you're welcome to join us."

"Thanks," I said, taking a tentative step further into the clearing.

His friend, a man maybe ten years younger that sat across from him – until I looked at his eyes and knew without a doubt he was the first man's son – smiled as well and pointed toward the very back corner. "Fred's free. I'm sure he wouldn't mind having someone to play with."

"Yes, Fred's always up for a challenge," the father said.

"Thank you," I said, and left them to their game.

My feet crunched in the cold leaves as I wound

my way around the tables. Some of the men looked up at me, some paid me no mind.

Fred, it seemed, had missed the fact that his name had been volunteered.

He didn't look up at me until I slid into the wooden bench seat across from him.

He was a man around Mr. Thompson's age, with a kindly face and grey hair that had been trimmed close to his head except on top, where some of the pewter curls spilled over onto his tall forehead. Said forehead wrinkled as he looked up at me through his oval spectacles, his grey eyes showing mild surprise and interest.

"How intriguing," he said, looking back down at the board. "I cannot remember the last time I played a young woman that was not my daughter. Perhaps I never have."

I shifted on the cold bench, trying to keep my fingers tucked inside the sleeves of my coat. "I'm... not here to play chess," I said.

That caused him to lift his eyes to me again. He stared at me over the top of his glasses, his face impassive. "Oh?"

"I'm Sheriff Hollis' sister," I said. "And I'm here to look for information."

He sat up away from the board, his lips pursing

with greater interest. "Are you, now?" he asked. He crossed his arms. "I take it this is for a police case of some sort?"

I nodded. "Would there be someone here who would be willing to answer a couple of questions I have about a person who frequents your chess group here?"

He inhaled deeply, burying his bare hands beneath the folds of his thick, cable knit sweater. "And who might that be?" he asked. "I won't volunteer anyone until I know what it is you're looking for."

I looked around, swallowing hard. My throat ached, but I couldn't be sure it wasn't from the chill in the air. "Mr. Thompson," I said. "He's...been missing."

His eyes flashed, and I knew at once that I'd managed to sit down with the right man.

Then it struck me.

"Was he your chess partner?"

The man nodded, exhaling as he leaned back onto the table on his elbows. "That he is. But you said *was*. Have you come down here to inform us of what we've all been wondering?"

My brow furrowed. "No, I – " I started. "I'm sorry. I realize my error with how I worded that." I remembered Roger giving me his blessing, and decided to run with it. "We have reason to believe that he might have gone missing, or maybe fallen ill. I found out that he liked to come down here to play chess, so I thought it was a good way to learn a little more about him."

Fred's eyes narrowed. "Why haven't you tried talking to his family? His son lives with him."

"I know he does," I said. "And he's not willing to discuss his father with us at all."

The muscles in his jaw clenched as he looked down, but he looked torn.

"You can tell me what you're thinking," I said. "I care about what's happened to him, too. He's our next door neighbor."

He studied me for a long, hard minute, his face as cold and stony as the marble chess table between us. "You're not lying to me?" he asked. "You're really the sheriff's sister?"

"I am," I said. "I'd say we could go down to the station and talk to him right now, but he's been busy getting things ready for Christmas. I decided to take this on to help lighten his load so he can enjoy some time with his boys."

"An admirable gesture," he said. "All right. Yes, Willard's a good friend of mine. Old friend. We both were born and raised here in Cobbsville. Don't think either of us has ever gone more than thirty miles outside this place."

My gaze narrowed. "...But?" I asked.

He looked away. "I'd still consider myself to be his friend, but lately, it seems that it's only me. He stopped coming down here to play with us months ago."

That long?

"I can't remember the last time I spoke with him, face to face," Fred said, and I could hear the regret in his voice.

"It seems that's the story these days," I said. "I don't know anyone who's spoken with him for some time."

Forehead wrinkling, he glowered at me. "You said he might have gone missing...Why do you think that?" he asked, his voice surprisingly steady.

"A myriad of reasons that I am not at liberty to discuss right now, unfortunately," I said. "Just know that he hasn't been snubbing you alone."

This clearly frustrated him, and I wondered if I should have been more open. *No, it's nothing more than speculation. Roger's right; if this sort of thing got back to him and everything's fine, then who knows what he or his son might end up trying to do. I don't like the idea of a defamation lawsuit or anything like it.*

"What can you tell me about your attempts to speak with him?" I asked. "You said you've been the only one trying lately. What did you mean?"

He shrugged, shaking his head. "I've stopped by his house, but I've never been able to get anyone to come to the door. First few times, I thought I just had bad luck, bad timing, whatever. But then it continued to happen. I tried calling the house, but no one would pick up."

"When did this happen?" I asked.

"Just in the last few months," he said. "I tried more earnestly before Thanksgiving, but since then, I've just given up. No one's heard anything from him, which we all found a little strange, but what could we do?"

Nothing, which is the trouble that we're running into, as well. "Did you get a chance to talk to his son?" I asked. "He's been there, taking care of some of the work around the house that I used to see his father doing."

He shook his head, his face turning sour. "Gerald, right?" His nose wrinkled, like a dog about to snarl. "I have great respect for Willard, and his late wife, but those kids of theirs...something went screwy."

A shiver trailed down my spine, and this time I knew it wasn't from the bitter air. "How do you mean?" I asked.

"Those kids, all three of them, never cared one lick for their parents. Never were grateful for how much Willard and Milly sacrificed for them. Bunch of selfish, good for nothing – they all left the minute they could, starting with their eldest, their daughter – looking for a better life elsewhere. Yet, to a one, each of them came crawling back home when their own life experiments failed."

"I'd been wondering why Gerald had moved in with his father," I said in a low voice.

"Each one, like the prodigal son – except none of them showed any sign of change. In fact, they all seemed worse off, chomping at the bit for their father to give it up and die already."

"Really?" I asked, hardly daring to believe it. *This sounds like a tall tale, but I can't think of anyone who cares anything for Gerald. They have a hard enough time liking Mr. Thompson who's lived there on Pine Street for so long.*

"Leeches, all three of them, concerned only for

themselves and what their father would eventually be leaving them," Fred said.

My eyes widened. "And he told you all this?"

He barked with a hollow laugh. "Told me? I already told you, Willard's a good friend of mine. I witnessed much of this with my own eyes." He sighed, some of his anger fading, like he didn't have the strength to keep it up. "Eventually, the two oldest abandoned Willard when he told them he wouldn't be giving them anything more to encourage their poor decisions. You see, his daughter was determined to throw her life away as an aspiring actress, though she never had any success, while his son had been arrested many times for involvement in an illegal gambling ring."

I wonder if that was here. And I wonder if it happened in Ricky Booker's basement.

Suddenly, some of Craig's wariness of his neighbors was starting to make more sense to me.

"But his youngest son...he just always struck me as a more bitter chip off the old block," Fred said poisonously.

"Gerald, you mean?" I asked.

He nodded.

I sighed. *Why is it that I am running into barriers*

on all sides? It's clear that everyone's worried, but that's still not proof that something needs to be looked into.

I decided I might need to dig a little harder.

Sorry, Fred.

"I don't mean to alarm you..." I said, dropping my voice; it seemed Fred's passionate frustrations had drawn the eye of a few of his companions. They'd since gone back to their games...or at least appeared to. "But we are concerned, just as you seem to be, that there is something going on in that household. Why would Mr. Thompson ever have reason to keep his son around if they dislike each other so much? Does he know something about his son that he's using as blackmail? Or maybe the other way around?"

Fred met my gaze with a steely expression that surprised me. Whatever this man had seen in his life, it had been hard enough that he could look me in the eye to discuss the possible gruesome end of one of his closest friends. "I don't know," he said after a long moment of contemplation. "But I hate to think there could be something terrible happening behind those closed doors. It troubles me that even you and your brother were unable to get in to see him. If they weren't hiding anything, they'd have no reason to bar anyone's entrance."

"That's our thought, as well," I said. I was becoming all the more grateful that I'd spoken with Roger about all this. At least I could sit and talk with Fred knowing that I had some support from the real authorities.

"Unfortunately, this is not the first time I've heard of such things," he said. "Evil breeds in the dark, right? Isn't that the old saying?"

"Something like that," I said.

He shook his head. "I just hate to see anything like this happen to my friend." He looked me hard in the eye again. "After losing Milly, he became…almost a different person."

"That happens to some people," I said.

I looked around, spying more than one pair watching us. As soon as they noticed my gaze, they swiftly turned back to their tables, pretending to play by arbitrarily snatching pieces off the board, or scratching their chins.

"I'm sorry to have come down here without better news to bring you," I said, getting to my feet. "I really wish I had answers for you."

"So do I," he said. "At this point, I'd just like someone to find out what's happening over there."

"That's the plan, sir, as soon as I find a good

enough reason to get in there and look around," I said. "Or, my brother, that is."

"Just...take caution with that Gerald, will you?" he said. "He's always been the quiet sort, but devious, too. I'm worried that he might just be pushing people around so he could get a rise out of them. That way, when he reacts defensively, it wouldn't be his fault."

"Antagonistic," I said, nodding. "That certainly sounds like him, if he's at all like his father."

"He's the type," Fred said. "He'd act like that just to get attention from his parents when he was younger. I don't want to jump to any conclusions, but...remember that he's had a history of it."

"I'll keep that in mind," I said. "And thank you, Fred."

He smiled, despite the heaviness in his eyes. "I'd sure like it if you came back one day and had a real game with me."

I smiled, too. "I'd like that. I can bring my nephews. Might do them some good to practice against someone other than me or their dad."

He chuckled. "I'll count on it, then."

I hesitated. "...And I'll do my best to find out what happened to your friend, okay? Hopefully it's nothing more than a big misunderstanding."

His smile faded, but he nodded. "I can certainly hope for it."

I headed back out of the park, ignoring the whispers that followed after me.

We certainly could hope for it…but that didn't mean we should expect it.

I must prepare for the worst, and hope for the best.

Why did it always seem that I never prepared thoroughly enough?

11

"Hey, Toby? Can you get the door for me?" I asked, balancing precariously on the end of Craig's old stepladder, trying my best to hang the last strand of garland over the doorway into the dining room.

The thought struck me after I'd gotten home from the park that there was an entire box of decorations that I'd never gotten to still up in the attic, and we only had a short time left to enjoy them. I might not have bothered, but still bound and determined to give the boys their best Christmas yet, I'd dragged it down and hastily begun to hang it all up as quickly as I could.

"You got it, Aunt Barbara," Toby called somewhere in the kitchen. I'd given him and Tim the task of untangling another strand of lights before they headed out to play across the street with Elaine and her brothers.

I managed to finish tapping the small nail into the wall just above the doorframe when I heard the door creak in the living room.

"Hey, Toby, is your aunt home?"

"Yeah, one second – Aunt Barbara! Mrs. Benson is here!"

I wobbled on the stepladder, glowering at the hanging garland on the other side of the doorframe. I sighed. "Coming!"

I climbed down, brushing some of the loose pine needles from my hair as I reached the door.

"Bye, Aunt Barb!" Tim exclaimed, shooting out the door. "Excuse me, Mrs. Benson!"

Toby scooted out right behind him. "Bye, Mrs. Benson! Bye, Aunt Barbara!"

"Bye, boys!" Mrs. Benson said.

"Be back before dinner in an hour!" I called to them.

Tim gave me a thumbs up over his head as he ran down the sloped front lawn.

I turned to Mrs. Benson, a pretty woman with thick auburn hair and wide hips. "Sorry about that," I said, smiling at her.

"Still decorating, huh?" she asked with a laugh.

I looked down and spotted the cluster of fallen needles that she'd caught sight of resting on my shoulder. "Oh, yes," I said, brushing them away. "Just a few things I forgot to do."

"It's hard to believe Christmas is only two days away," she said with a sigh. "Seems like it comes faster every year."

"It sure does..." I said. A moment of silence lapsed between us as we heard shouts from the kids across the street; they'd probably met the others out in their backyard. They essentially had permission to come and go as they pleased from the Foster's. "So...what can I help you with?" I asked.

"I'm sorry to bother you, but I've been going door to door, saw you were home, and thought I'd take a chance," she said. Worry creased her brow. "You haven't seen our dog, by any chance, have you?"

"Dixie?" I asked, then shook my head. "A big brown dog, right? No, I haven't seen her lately."

She sighed, her shoulders sagging. "I've been looking for her for almost an hour now. She took off when she saw the mailman delivering a huge stack of boxes to the Parkers down the street, and I haven't been able to find her."

"Oh, I'm sorry," I said. "I'll definitely keep an eye

out, though. I can go run over and ask the boys if they've seen her – "

She shook her head. "That's okay, I was heading over there to ask Vicky if she's seen her. Sometimes she likes to drink out of the birdbath in the Foster's garden. If you do see her, just give me a call! I should be home tonight and tomorrow getting ready for Christmas."

"Sure thing," I said.

She glanced next door as she turned. "I stopped by Mr. Thompson's house and tried to ask for their help, but his son just…shooed me away."

I froze, staring at her concerned face as she looked across our yard and into theirs.

She shook her head, looking at me with frustration and worry. "One of the few things that Mr. Thompson has always loved is dogs. It's the one thing I've always seen him happy about. Prefers them to people, I suppose. He would even have special dog treats that he'd give to the neighbors and their dogs when he'd see them walking by."

"Really?" I asked.

"Really," she said. "You wouldn't know it by how he acts now, but when his wife was still alive, he'd sit out on that porch and talk to everyone as they passed by the house. Sure, he's always been a little distant, likes to keep to himself. I know it's been hard on him these last few years after her passing..." Then she scowled again. "But why is it that his son is acting the exact opposite, not even wanting to help me?"

"I don't know..." I said.

"I don't know, either," she said, exasperated. "For some reason, it just seems like he wants to shut us all out and away from his poor father. I feel sorry for the man."

She sighed, then smiled over her shoulder at me.

"Well, anyway, if you see the dog, give me a holler, would you?"

"Happy to do so," I said, and watched her meander down our drive toward the Foster's.

It seemed strange to me that Mrs. Benson had the first differing opinion about Mr. Thompson. Everyone said that he'd changed since his wife had died, and so I guessed I should have realized that he might not have been so nasty beforehand.

He had good friends that he saw regularly. A man with a nasty attitude wouldn't be able to keep friends for very long.

It did surprise me that he loved dogs, and he'd even interact with the neighbors. *Special treats for the dogs, huh?*

I shouldn't have been surprised that Gerald would have turned her away at the door, but it still irked me that he wouldn't even be willing to help.

This is getting ridiculous. The entire town is wondering what in the world is happening in that house, and we are no closer to figuring it out.

If it wasn't for the fact that Gerald continued to answer the door, if only to send people away, I might have thought that there wasn't anyone even in the house in the first place.

I closed the door behind myself, forgetting the hanging garland in the dining room for a few minutes.

It doesn't seem to matter how much I try to ignore Mr. Thompson. It just keeps coming back to haunt me.

I hoped not literally.

I sighed, glancing up at the clock.

Like clockwork, Gerald would be sure to take the trash out to the garbage can behind the house. Every day at four o'clock, he'd kick open the screen door at the back of the house, the obnoxious creak being what often drew my attention. The sound seemed especially harsh in these cool temperatures. He'd slump around the side of the house, deposit a single bag of garbage, not more than half full, into the receptacle, then make his way back inside. Just like he had that day when I'd had my garden party, though that had been an odd time of day. I couldn't remember him ever stepping foot outside the house that early in the day apart from going to collect the morning paper.

I chewed the inside of my lip. I wondered if he *knew* just how aggravating it must have been for me, to watch him, day in and day out, not knowing anything more than what my own eyes could tell me.

He probably has no idea that you have even the faintest interest in what's happening in his house, I chastised myself. *He's probably oblivious that he and his father have garnered the attention of half the neighborhood, as well as the police department.*

Maybe it was best that he didn't know. If – no, *when* – we were able to do something, *when* we finally found that key piece of information that would give Craig and Roger the excuse to go in, then he'd know.

And I couldn't help but feel a little bit excited about it. I knew that was wrong, but he had been the cause of a lot of my consternation in the last few weeks, and I was about ready to have it done.

Could I sound more selfish?

But all I wanted was an answer about him, about *why* Gerald was so reluctant to share anything about his father. No one seemed to know what in the world was going on, and I couldn't just break in and see for myself; Craig and Roger had been perfectly clear that I was not to go anywhere near the house. So far, I'd been a good girl and listened to them.

Now, I snuck around our house and into the garage, taking a post at the side window that overlooked our side yard. Through the row of trees that separated our yard from the Thompson's, I could just see the trash can.

Sure enough, the screen door swung outward and out tramped Gerald.

What if he did know what everyone was whispering about him?

What if he does...and he's relishing in it? Doing this on purpose?

Just like Fred, Mr. Thompson's friend from the park, had warned me. *He said Gerald was the sort to push people around just to get a rise out of them.*

It might be one way for him to get some attention from his neighbors. It made me think of the kids in school that would act out just to be noticed by the other students and the teachers, even if that sort of recognition only ever got them into trouble.

Didn't Fred say Gerald was the youngest? Typically, the youngest children were the ones to receive the most attention, along with the most resistance from parents about growing up. As such, they'd become spoiled, selfish, and sometimes outright rotten. Some would get anything they wanted.

I wrinkled my nose, gripping my arms that I'd folded over my body to keep myself from bolting out the back door and chasing Gerald down.

I watched him pause, and turn to glance over his shoulder.

Icy fear exploded in my chest, and I spun out of sight, shielding myself against the wall of the garage.

My breath came in short bursts as I chanced a look back outside a few moments later, and managed to catch sight of the back door swinging shut again.

Breathing a sigh of relief, I headed back inside.

This was a possibility I hadn't considered, but it might have been one worth sharing with Roger. Fred thought Gerald to be antagonistic; what if he was trying to upset everyone in the neighborhood so much that eventually someone might just become angry enough with his vagueness and fly off the handle at him? That way he'd have the excuse to react equally in anger, maybe even going so far as to take legal action.

I thought that was what Roger had seemed concerned about.

I could almost see the sly little smirk on Gerald's face, just *waiting* for someone to challenge him; a bear hoping to be poked so it could attack.

It was like a game of stalemates, waiting for the first person to strike.

Would it be me? Roger? Or would it be Gerald?

Something did not feel right about the whole thing. I had begun to really worry about old Mr. Thompson.

Christmas was two days away. Could I really afford to try and unravel all of this now?

But if I don't, and something happens next door in that time...then will it be too late?

How could I know?

I groaned out loud, knotting my hands in my hair.

What if it already was too late?

The door burst open, and I let out a yelp as a blur of a figure came dashing inside, followed by a second one.

It wasn't until a shriek of laughter followed that I realized it was Tim and Toby.

I pressed a hand to my thundering heart. "Welcome back, boys..." I said, going to close the door behind them.

"What's the matter, Aunt Barbara?" Tim asked.

"Yeah, why do you look like you've seen a ghost?" Toby added.

"I haven't," I said, glowering at the pair of them. "What made you think it was a good idea to come running in here like that?"

Toby and Tim exchanged a look. "We always do that," Toby said, his brow furrowing. Then a devious smile took its place. "Let me guess, you were talking with *Deputy Elwood* on the phone, weren't you? And we caught you?"

My face flushed scarlet. "I – what? No, I wasn't – "

Tim grinned at me while his brother threw back his head and laughed.

"Hey!" I said, my hands balling into fists. "I wasn't even on the telephone!"

"Maybe not now, but were you after Mrs. Benson left?" Tim asked.

"No," I said, flatly starting off toward the kitchen. "Now, wash up for dinner, the both of you. Your father should be home soon."

Toby whistled through his teeth, following after me into the kitchen.

I heard him snicker beside me while I turned the oven off.

"What's so funny?" I asked, probably more curtly than I should have. I hardly felt guilty, though; it wasn't like I'd asked them to frighten the life out of me when I was so lost in my thoughts.

"You and the deputy," Toby sniggered. "We saw you two at the Christmas party. Like a couple of love birds." He fluttered his eyelashes at me.

"Stop that," I said, my face burning; it was a good thing I had ducked down to grab the casserole out of the oven. "There was nothing like that going on."

"Quick to deny it," Toby said to his brother, chortling even more.

I set the casserole down with a loud clatter, turning to glare at them, my eyes narrowing. "If you knew what was good for you, you'd stop this right now. Didn't your father ever teach you anything about privacy?"

"I think we've touched a nerve," Toby said.

"Deputy Elwood is a really nice guy," Tim said. "You don't have to be embarrassed if you like him. In fact, we sort of expected that eventually you'd – "

"Out of the kitchen, both of you," I said, snatching a kitchen towel and snapping it at their shins. "Out, out, out! Go get your hands washed. Now!"

They bent their heads together, shooting one last look at me over their shoulders, before disappearing into the living room.

I heaved a sigh, tossing the towel onto the counter.

They were wrong. Completely wrong.

It was nothing more than annoyance that had left my cheeks as hot as they were.

12

The day before Christmas Eve dawned much warmer than the days before. The sun blazed through the window, burning off any of the chill that had settled over the valley and low mountains of Cobbsville. It didn't seem to dampen the Christmas cheer, though, as the boys woke before they usually did with wild anticipation that only children can have so close to Christmas.

"Aunt Barbara, can we bake more cookies?" Toby asked.

"Are there any other presents that you need to wrap?" Tim asked.

"What about any shopping? I kind of want to see just how busy the stores are today – " Toby started before I laid a hand on his shoulder, laughing.

"Slow down, boys. I understand that you're excited, but we don't need to try and do everything all at once," I said, glancing between the two of them. "Now, I do have some plans for the day, and *one* errand I need to run. I have to go to the grocery store – "

"Can we come with you?" Toby asked eagerly.

"Maybe," I said. "It depends on when your dad is going to be getting back from the station – "

"What's this?" Craig asked, wandering into the kitchen while he buttoned the cuffs of his brown sheriff's uniform. "Why are you badgering your aunt now?"

"They want to go with me to the grocery store," I said.

"No, I don't think so," Craig said, grabbing his cup of coffee I'd left for him on the counter. "Not a good idea."

"But Dad – "

"No buts, Tim," he said, with the calm and collected demeanor of a man who had a great deal of practice telling his sons *no*." "I'm only taking a half day today, as long as nothing comes up – "

Expectedly, Toby glowered at his father. "Aw, come on, Dad, you can't be serious about taking any new jobs today, right?"

"You promised us that you'd be here this year," Tim added, bowing his head, mumbling into his chest.

"I know, and I intend to be," Craig answered, looking Toby and then Tim straight in the eyes. "I have no reason to believe that anything will happen, but I can't predict emergencies."

I turned away. I had planned to call Roger to try and see what he thought I should do, if anything. I'd really hoped to have had a final answer to what was the issue over in the Thompson house before Christmas, but I had a hard time seeing a way to finish it now.

I could only hope that nothing *would* happen over there until Christmas had come and gone.

I wish it was already over. I hate the idea of this thing hanging over my head like it is. I don't want it to ruin my first Christmas here.

"But what if Aunt Barbara needs our help?" Toby asked.

"She won't," Craig said. "It will be better for her to get in and out rather than having you both underfoot asking for any number of things you don't need."

"Aww…" Toby said.

In truth, I was glad that he had said as much. It

was the same thing I'd thought, but I hadn't wanted to disappoint the boys.

"All right, you two, behave today while I'm gone," Craig said. "Sorry to have my coffee and run, Barb. I just want to get all the last minute things done before it gets too late, you know?"

"Get going, then," I said with a dismissive wave. "Stop yacking with me and get yourself back here in good time, okay?"

He smiled at me. "If you need anything, I'll be at the office until around noon, one at the latest – "

"*Dad!*" Toby whined. "You said you'd be home for lunch!"

"I will!" Craig said with a laugh. "Just call it a late lunch, okay?"

"Dad..." he groaned.

Craig reached over and went to ruffle Toby's hair, but the boy ducked out from underneath.

A wry grin spread across Toby's face, but his eyes grew wide when his dad bent down himself, arms stretching out like a snake attacking, and grabbed hold of Toby around the waist.

He shrieked as Craig hoisted him into the air in one smooth motion over his shoulder, and took off into the living room.

Toby laughed and squealed as if he was five years old again, and all I could do was smile.

"Dad, *Dad!* Put me *down!*" Toby shrieked in between gasps of laughter.

Tim just shook his head, smiling up at me. "Works every time," he said.

We said goodbye to their dad a short time later, and they both settled down to clean their room – under direct order from their father.

"You don't know what *Santa Claus* might be bringing you," he said. "And I want to make sure that we have room for all the – "

"Dad! We know you're Santa!" Tim said.

"That changes nothing," Craig said. "Now, I give your aunt full permission to scold you and tell me if you aren't behaving. I love you both."

"We love you too, Dad!"

I stood by in the door to their room for a good five minutes before we all realized that there would be no real cleaning done in that room. "Just don't make more of a mess in here, okay?" I said. I didn't have the heart to make them do more housework the day before Christmas.

Still, as I wandered around the house, picking things up, I heard the two of them talking and laughing together, along with the sound of shifting items. I wanted to take a peek, curious as to their progress, but resisted. If they wanted me to see it, they'd call –

A muffled sound in the distance gave me pause.

Ordinarily, it was the sort of noise I'd ignore entirely. Really, it shouldn't have caught my attention, but because of what happened the day before...

"Hey, is that Dixie?" Tim called out from their room.

I listened hard, barely daring to breathe.

It was almost inaudible, but I heard the sound again.

"I think it might be," I said. "You boys stay here, all right? I'm going to go take a peek outside."

I reached for my jacket, but as soon as I pulled open the door, I realized that I didn't really need it. Humidity made me regret putting on corduroy pants that morning, which would surely chafe as soon as sweat started to form, but I knew it wouldn't be this way for long; the rolling, dark clouds in the east told me that there must have been a large storm cell coming in off the direction of the sea. *Must be coming in over the mountains...*

The barking echoed down the street, bouncing off the houses, distorting the sound.

I hoped that Mrs. Benson had heard what I had.

Outside, I made my way down to the end of the driveway, looking down the length of the street, hoping to catch sight of the large dog. It'd be hard to miss her, given her excitement whenever she made eye contact with anyone. If she spotted a neighbor she knew, she'd take off for them without hesitation.

It made me wonder if that was why Mrs. Benson didn't seem altogether *that* worried about the dog. This must have happened before.

I paused, straining to hear what I could above the wind that had started to pick up.

I hadn't seen a flash of caramel-colored fur yet, but that didn't mean that she hadn't wandered behind one of the nearby cars sitting in the driveways of our neighbors.

Oh, come on, Dixie. I don't want to have to spend the next hour looking for you –

"Hey, Barbara!"

Vicky hurried up her driveway, tugging her arm through a sweater sleeve. Her apron tied around her waist, bespeckled with molasses and brown sugar, swayed in the wind.

"Hi, there," I said, glancing down the street for the cars that were never coming, but that I checked for out of habit all the same. "You look like you've been busy today."

She flashed me a brief smile. "I thought I heard Dixie."

"I thought I did, too," I said.

"I take it you haven't see her yet?" she asked, reaching down to wipe some flour off her hands onto her apron.

"No," I said. "Have you?"

She shook her head, too.

"Maybe she's just up the road a bit here," I said, starting in that direction.

She quickly glanced over her shoulder before she hurried up beside me. "I can't be gone long," she said. "I've got some cookies ready to bake before Robert and the kids get back."

"I'm sure it won't be too long," I said.

Vicky grabbed hold of my arm when we heard another bark from down the street – at least, we thought it was down the street.

But it wasn't. It was next door.

Our heads swiveled around in the direction of the barking.

An icy chill ran down my spine.

"Mr. Thompson's yard..." I breathed, looking over at Vicky.

She frowned, worry creasing her brow. "You don't think she's actually back there, do you? Maybe she's in the Mitchell's yard?"

I swallowed hard. "Maybe…" I said.

I didn't really know what to do. I didn't want to walk up to the Thompson's house, worried that Gerald or his father might see us coming. I didn't fancy the idea of getting an earful from the son, nor trying to get his permission to go check the backyard for the dog if he wouldn't.

"We can't just go onto their property," Vicky said, echoing my thoughts.

"No…" I said. "But there's definitely another way. Do you feel like checking it out with me?"

She searched my face for a second. "What do you mean?"

"Come on," I said.

We made our way up the drive and back into the house.

"Maybe we should just call Mrs. Benson and let her know," Vicky said.

"It might not be Dixie," I said. "I'd hate to send her all the way over here just to find out that it wasn't, or to have either of the Thompsons stop her from looking."

I passed through the kitchen, and onto the back porch.

"Oh, I see," she said, coming up beside me.

From our back porch, we had a decent view of the Thompson's backyard. Some of it remained hidden behind the fence and row of bushes on their side, but all things considered, we could see much of it.

"Good idea," Vicky said under her breath, tucking her hands beneath her arms, ducking her head as if hiding in plain sight. "We can watch from here."

"And they can't get mad if they spot us," I said.

She smiled at me.

"So...I guess we wait?" I asked. "For the dog to – "

I was interrupted by sharp barking sounds.

A chill swept through me. Vicky and I glanced at each other.

"That was definitely from their yard, wasn't it?" I murmured.

"Oh, it certainly was," she answered, squinting as she stared out over the fence.

"Over there!" she said, grabbing my arm with one hand, pointing with the other.

My eyes followed to the line of trees leading into the forest behind the house, up the same hill that our home butted up against. The trees grew dense just beyond the houses. The boys often wandered up there, following along some of the paths that they and Craig had worn down over the years exploring the few acres they owned.

"Maybe we could take some of those paths up and around behind the house," I said. "What could they really do if we were to come back onto their property from that way?"

"No, over there! I see her!" Vicky hissed, tugging me down a few inches, pointing more fervently. "See?"

I peered through a gap in the line of trees and gasped.

I'd missed the dog entirely because the caramel color of her fur had blended in all too well with the southern oak trunks around her. I could see her now, though, hunched over and –

"Is she...digging?" I asked.

"That's what it looks like," Vicky said.

I straightened. "Dixie!" I called, as loud as I dared. "Hey, Dixie! Come here, girl! Come here!"

The dog did not stop in her fervent extraction of whatever it was that she found so enticing in the ground.

"Oh, for Pete's sake...she's probably trying to dig up a mole or something," I said, pressing my hands to my hips.

"Dixie!" Vicky shouted.

"Shh!" I hissed, grabbing her and pulling her back from the edge of the deck. "We don't want the Thompsons to hear us!"

Dixie did look up at that, though. For a brief second, she stared in our direction.

"I know she sees us," I said. "That dog's not dumb."

"No, but that means she's ignoring us," Vicky said.

"Maybe we should go call Mrs. Benson now," I said.

"We can't just walk away," Vicky said. "What if she takes off again? We can *see* her. We should go get her."

"Are you crazy?" I asked.

"Well, what other suggestion do you have?" she asked. "We don't exactly have many options, especially when the dog's not listening to us."

I stared out over the yard. Dixie had returned to pulverizing the edge of the forest once more.

"You're right..." I said. "We might have to drag her away from whatever it is she's found."

"When she gets stuck on something, she'll chase it," Vicky said.

"Hence the mailman, and the running away..." I said with a sigh. "All right... If we are going to do this, then we need to go *quietly.* If they catch us in their yard, there's no telling what they might do. I have no idea the mental state of those men inside that house, and don't know if they'd be too pleased to see us sneaking through their backyard."

"I know what you man," she said.

I raised my eyebrows. "And you still want to go?"

"I want to make sure our friend and her family get their dog back for Christmas," Vicky said. "Come on, it won't be that bad."

"All right," I said. "But let's not dawdle, okay? Grab the dog, drag her back over to our yard, into the truck, and down to the Benson's."

"We can do this!" Vicky said, nodding.

I wasn't so sure I agreed. "I appreciate your confidence," I said.

I started down the steps of the back porch and into the yard, Vicky following close behind. I didn't really know why I felt the need to tread as carefully through our yard as I did other than I wanted the practice ahead of time. My muscles tensed as we drew nearer to the gap in the fence, a board that had broken down after a particularly bad thunderstorm in early September, that no one had taken the time to fix yet.

Heart pounding, I paused at the threshold,

glancing toward the Thompson house. As usual, it remained dark, lifeless.

What was I really scared of? Gerald or Mr. Thompson coming out of the house to shout at me? Mr. Thompson had gone after the boys a handful of times, waving his cane in the air. They might get wide-eyed when they shared those memories, but they were kids.

I was a grown woman, wasn't I? Couldn't I handle this?

Yes, I could. And I would.

I curled my hands into fists and stepped over the border.

The crunch of the dried winter leaves sent shivers down my spine, and immediately I ceased moving. I hadn't taken even one full step into the Thompson yard before I considered turning back.

"Are you okay?" Vicky whispered behind me.

"Yes," I murmured back. "Just – looking around."

It was not altogether a lie, but not the real truth, either.

I hadn't confronted the Thompsons. All this time, everyone else seemed to be doing it for me. After the time Vicky and I had spoken with Gerald, all my observations about the house and the family had been just that; observation.

Now, standing in their yard, the knots in my stomach twisted tighter. I might as well have been wandering through their living room, as intrusive as this seemed.

Dixie continued to scrounge in the dirt on the far side of the yard, happily ignoring us and our approach. This close to their back porch, I didn't dare raise my voice above a whisper. Besides, trying to call out to her might spook her and send her running again.

Might be best to try and sneak up on her, too.

Not much good that would do, though, as she'd already caught sight of us before we came over.

I started toward one of the southern oaks with a wide trunk that skirted along the back of the yard. It required a few moments of being out in the open yard, with the sunlight beaming down on me from above like a giant spotlight, but I managed to make it.

Vicky, likewise, came right after me, following my footsteps as closely as a mime would.

We huddled behind the tree for a moment.

This was more difficult than I thought it would be. Still, we were already here, already committed to the idea.

We might as well see it through.

All for some dumb dog...

I thought of Mrs. Benson's face, and the worry I knew her kids must feel.

No...not a dumb dog. She might be stubborn, but she's not dumb.

We just needed to resolve this.

I really did *not* need this additional stress.

I drew in a deep breath. "Come on," I whispered, and ducked out from behind the tree again.

We continued along the length of the yard much in the same way. Pausing behind the trees, searching the yard, taking quiet looks at the back porch to make sure we weren't being watched.

"It's possible they aren't even home," Vicky muttered hopefully from our hiding spot about halfway across the yard. "We could be doing all this hiding for nothing."

"That's true," I said. "But I don't really want to walk out in the open and find out."

Vicky's nose screwed up. "No, I guess I don't either."

A large tree with sprawling limbs obstructed our view of Dixie, but I knew she remained fixed to that spot because of the dirt spraying out from behind the trunk.

Dragging her back through the yard might prove

to be difficult, especially if she wanted to go back to digging at that spot.

She must have buried something there over the past few days. That's why she's come back here.

I pursed my lips. Would Vicky and I be able to pull a dog as big as she was away? She must have weighed close to eighty pounds, if not more. Wouldn't she be able to break free of our hold with one good burst of speed?

I really needed to stop sabotaging myself with these sorts of questions!

I collected myself for just a moment, knowing that the sooner we got to her, the sooner we could get out of here.

I stepped out from behind the tree when the sound of a door slamming shut sent me scrambling back for cover.

Heart hammering against my ribs, I peered out from behind the tree back toward Mr. Thompson's house. The door at the back didn't appear to be open, and there was no sign of Gerald anywhere.

I crouched behind the tree like a frightened rabbit, my hands gripping the rough bark as if I might sprout claws and be able to scale it if danger should arise.

Vicky, face pale and eyes wide, nodded toward

the yard beside the Thompson's. Mr. Mitchell carried an armful of empty boxes toward his fire pit, likely leftover from wrapping Christmas packages.

I let out a breath I'd been holding.

"Let's get this over with..." I muttered.

I hurried out from behind the tree, my fresh desire to finish the task at hand outweighing the fear of being caught by Gerald or his father.

"Dixie!" I hissed as we drew nearer. "Quit that! Get over here!"

The dog looked up at me, making full eye contact before she resumed her ferocious digging.

"Oh for goodness' sake – " I said, starting toward her.

"What's she pulling at?" Vicky asked.

Dixie, ducking her head, definitely seemed to have found whatever it was she had been looking for. She tugged and tugged, and when she shifted to the side to try and get better footing, I realized it was a shoe.

"You came over here to unbury a shoe?" I asked. "Well, I'm sure Mrs. Benson will be pleased to know that we've found both her dog and one of her family's missing shoes."

Dixie remained entirely aloof to us, intent on unearthing that treasure of hers.

"She's not going to give up on this, is she?" Vicky asked.

"No, probably not," I said. "Fine."

I drew nearer, glaring at the back of the dog's head. Why was she having such a difficult time pulling it out of the ground? It was just a shoe.

She must have buried it really well.

"It looks like its caught on a root or something – " I started.

And then I froze where I stood. The whole world seemed to stop, right then and there.

It didn't matter that the sun beat down on the back of my neck, or that the blue sky shone so bright despite the dark clouds that filled the sky in the east.

That's no tree root...

It was an ankle.

13

"Barbara?"

I barely heard Vicky. An odd ringing in my ears made it hard to think about anything apart from the shoe that Dixie tried desperately to dislodge from the ground.

With a sickening drop of my stomach, my gaze passed over the earth at my feet. Darker, richer, sparse compared to the dirt around it. *Somewhat freshly dug.*

My insides convulsed and I wheeled around.

Vicky's brow had knit together. "Barbara, what is it?"

"It's – " I said, but froze as a fuzzy shape behind her solidified in my sight.

Skin crawling, I straightened. I tried to swallow, but my whole mouth had gone dry.

"What's the – " Vicky asked, turning to follow my gaze. Her mouth fell open. "Gerald. Hi!"

Gerald Thompson stood at the edge of the tree line, hands hanging limply at his side, his face slack, gaze fixed squarely upon us.

"Dixie…Dixie, stop it," I hissed over my shoulder, waving a hand behind my back. "Go! Get!"

"It's all right," Gerald said, sliding his hands into the pockets of his plain, navy buttoned sweater. "I knew that someone would learn the truth eventually. Just thought I had more time."

I blinked at him, too horrified to look over my shoulder at the mound that held a body.

And there was only one person that could have been buried there.

"The truth?" Vicky asked with a chuckle. "Oh, it's – it's nothing like that. We don't know anything, honest. We just heard the Benson's dog out here and came over to try and coax dear old Dixie back home – "

"I know," he said. "If anyone did know, they would have been back here digging up my yard. I figured I was still safe." Then he ran his hands over the back of his neck. "Guess I should have anticipated a dog. Never crossed my mind."

I swallowed. This was not the way I thought this would go. Any of it.

"You...you did this?" I asked, hardly able to keep my voice steady.

"Buried my father?" he asked. "Yes, I did."

Vicky gasped. "Your – " It must have finally dawned on her what was happening. Terrified, shallow breathing began beside me, but I couldn't afford to look at her or try and comfort her.

I could hardly believe how things were unfolding myself.

"Did you..." I started.

Gerald's head tilted to the side, his face blank.

"Did you kill him?" I breathed.

His brow furrowed. "Kill my father? No. Of course I didn't."

"Liar." The word slipped out before I had even considered it fully.

He shook his head. "I'm telling the truth. He died of natural causes weeks ago. Almost a month, now, I think."

I just stared at him, dumbfounded.

Question after question rushed through my

mind, and for a second, I tried to ask three of them at once. "How – why didn't – what – "

"Come with me," he said, turning back toward the house. "I'll explain everything."

Neither Vicky nor I moved.

He paused, looking around at us. When he pulled his hand from his pocket, both Vicky and I jumped.

But then, he unfurled his hand, and five dog treats rolled forward onto his fingers. "You too, girl. Come here. Treats."

Finally, Dixie seemed to relent in her pursuit of the buried shoe, dashing over to Gerald with a happy bark.

"Shh, shh," Gerald said, dropping a treat on the ground at his feet. "Good girl. Don't need you getting all worked up again."

I eyed him nervously.

"Look, you can even use my telephone to call your brother," Gerald said. "While we wait, I'll explain everything to you."

Why, though? Why tell us anything?

He stared as blankly at me as I did at him. "Wouldn't your brother want someone to keep an eye on me so I don't run? You caught me, fair and square. I won't try to get away."

Still, I didn't move.

Vicky's fearful gaze pressed against the side of my face, willing me to look over at her, but I couldn't. Not yet. Not until I made a decision.

I shot a quick look over at our yard. It would be much better for us to go back to my own house and call Craig there. Out of Gerald's reach. After all, who knew if he was telling the truth about not being a murderer?

"Why didn't you tell us that your father was dead when we stopped by a few days ago?" I asked.

"I'll explain everything inside – "

"No," I said. "You tell me here."

He stared at me for a moment, then shrugged. "Oh, well. It's your own choice not to get a call in to your brother as soon as possible. Like I said, we could have this conversation inside after you called him."

"Why didn't you tell us?" I repeated.

"Because then I'd have to report my father dead," he said. "And that would mean having to give up the pension checks I've been collecting on his behalf."

"His...pension checks?" Vicky asked in a low voice.

"You didn't tell anyone your father was dead because you wanted his money?" I asked.

He nodded. "It's really not all that difficult to understand. Now, would you please accompany me back inside?"

I didn't move. I couldn't...not even with the knowledge that there was a month-old body behind me in a shallow, hand dug grave.

"You know the truth, now. I can't escape. I know that. I figured I'd get caught eventually. I promise I won't try and run. But if you go, then I will. I'll dig up the body and take it with me, and all you'll have is your word for what you've seen."

Now he was making idle threats? Surely he couldn't dig up and carry off a dead body that quickly. Still...could I risk it?

"Fine," I said. "We'll come with you."

"Good," he said, starting back toward his house. "It'll be good to get this off my chest. That, and we can call Mrs. Benson about her dog. That's right, good girl." He coaxed the dog along and up onto the porch with him.

I glared at the back of his head before following him.

Vicky reached out and grabbed hold of my sleeve. "Are you sure it's all right?" she breathed.

I hesitated. "Unfortunately, I think he made a good point," I said. "If we don't follow him, he could flee. We know – we know the truth." That was difficult to admit. "We'll simply call my brother and he'll be here in a few minutes."

"Right…" she said. She squared her shoulders. "Okay. Besides, there's two of us and one of him, right?"

"Right," I said, but turned away since we both knew that it was hardly an advantage.

Still…I'd been in this sort of situation before. I had faced danger head on like this.

But now you have Vicky to protect…and Roger isn't here to help you…

I pushed those thoughts away and climbed up onto Mr. Thompson's back porch.

I never imagined the inside of the Thompson household to smell like garlic, but it did, and a lot of it. The smell was overpowering, really, so much so that I had to resist pulling my shirt up over my nose to block the scent.

Everything seemed neat and tidy, however, at least at first glance; the mail lay on a table near the front door, stacked in a neat pile…but it must have been several weeks' worth. Clothes had been folded and sorted by color beside a basket on the dining room table…but that much folding must have taken hours, and only a small spot at the head of the table had been left open to use for its intended purpose of eating at. The living room must have been recently picked up, as there was nothing on the couch or the armchair, the fireplace mantle, the walls, or even anything on the bookshelf in the corner.

"What a lovely tree you have, Gerald," Vicky said nervously, eyeing the spindly, bare tree with a handful of lights feebly glowing upon it. It couldn't have been more than three feet high, though it appeared taller from its perch atop the television set. I supposed Vicky's natural politeness had prompted her to compliment it.

He shrugged. "Thought it needed something festive in here," he said. "After all, this was my mother's favorite holiday." He patted the couch beside him, calling Dixie up onto it. She obliged, and he gave her another treat. She sank down onto the cushions, chewing happily.

He turned to us, and both Vicky and I stopped. I made certain we were out of arm's reach.

"You see...Dad fell ill about six months ago. Went to the doctor. They said it was cancer."

"Oh, I knew it..." Vicky said under her breath beside me.

"He told the doctors that he didn't want treatment at his age. Said he'd rather die at home than in a hospital somewhere all hooked up to tubes and medicine. 'If I'm going to die in my sleep, it better be in my own bed,' is what he told them."

I sighed. "I guess I can't really blame him."

"I assume the doctors said he wouldn't live long?" Vicky asked tentatively, balling her hands up in front of herself.

"That's right," Gerald said. "They said he had a few months at best. He told me the house was mine if I stayed here and helped see him through to the end."

I blanched. Why did I have such a difficult time believing Gerald would do something so noble?

"But then why didn't you tell anyone when he died?" I asked. That was the big question. It was what confused me so deeply.

He shrugged. "I already told you. I wanted the pension checks."

I stared at him. "You know that's fraud, don't you?" I asked.

He shrugged. "I needed the money. I hoped to get a few months out of it before I got caught and came clean. Figured I would be able to claim at least through March. Then I'd tell the authorities what happened and maybe only have to give a few of the checks back. They come every week, you see."

"So you just...carried your dad's body out back and buried him yourself? In secret?" I asked. "Just like that?"

"Essentially," Gerald said. "It actually took me a day or two to notice that he was gone."

I shook my head, looking at him.

His expression remained blank, as uninterested as I'd ever seen him. *Maybe I mistook his indifference for fear or guilt that day we came to talk to him.*

"When did you decide to start keeping the checks?" I asked.

"Oh, I figured that out before he died," he said. "He told me that I'd only get a little while he was alive, since he'd signed over the rest of his savings to charities and the church after he was gone. Well, what he doesn't know won't hurt him, will it?"

"But you said he left you the house," I said, brow furrowing. "You could have just sold the house, made some money that way – "

"I had every intention of doing that," he said with a nod. "I'm not as dumb as I look, you know."

I wasn't suggesting that –

"I just wanted to save up a little bit of money before I moved on, is all," he said. "After everything my father did to me, after the way he treated me... taking a little of his money off the top wouldn't hurt.

What's a couple thousand dollars when I have my whole life ahead of me?"

"So let me get this straight..." I said. I needed a clear story to tell Craig and Roger. "Your dad died of cancer here at home. You buried him in the backyard, but didn't alert anyone because you wanted to keep collecting his weekly pension checks. You planned to tell everyone after some months had passed, and lie about how long he was actually dead."

He nodded. "That's about right, yes."

"You know you could go to jail," I said. "Even if you didn't kill him, you were still concealing a death, cashing a deceased person's checks, and taking his money."

"What good would that money do him? He's dead," Gerald said blankly.

"It doesn't matter; it's still fraud. It's theft," I said.

"I realize," he said.

Well, really, that was all I needed.

I didn't know why knowing the truth didn't make me feel any better. It was just sitting in my stomach like I'd swallowed an egg whole.

"All right, I guess I'll go call my brother," I said. "Where can I find your telephone?"

"Just one minute," he said. "Do you mind

following me up to the attic? There's something I'd like to show you there."

"I really should call my brother, first," I said.

He nodded. "It'll be just a few minutes. Please?"

Vicky shifted nervously beside me.

I licked my lips. So far, things had gone just like he said they would. He had told us everything, seemingly sparing no detail.

"What is it?" I asked. "What do you want to show us?"

"The checks," he said. "I still have most of them. I cashed a few, but the last three or four that came while he was still alive are up there. You can give them to your brother as proof."

My eyes narrowed. "Why are you so determined to sink yourself?" I asked.

He shrugged. "It was never my intention to let this get so out of hand, but clearly, it has. I'm going to set things right in hopes of a lighter punishment. Is that really so difficult to believe?"

The small hairs at the nape of my neck sprang up again. Something still didn't feel right.

He started for the stairs, which were just through the open doorway into the dark front hall behind him. "Come on, you should get home before it starts to storm."

"Let's just get this over with," Vicky said in a low voice beside me.

I nodded, and followed after him.

Access to the attic seemed to be the same here as it was at our house; an ordinary door stood at the end of the hall, and opening it up revealed a narrow set of wooden stairs leading up. Gerald flicked on a lonely bulb swinging just over his head, and started up.

Vicky reached out and grabbed hold of my sleeve, shaking it with a burst of worry before we followed him up. Dixie had remained downstairs, seemingly happy to lounge on the sofa while she waited for us.

"They're over here," he said, gesturing at the top of the stairs.

We might as well have wandered into a used furniture outlet. A wicker patio set stood in one corner, and an old couch draped in a tattered sheet loomed beside it. An old wardrobe missing a door, a trio of dining room chairs, and a number of wooden crates were scattered around. Dust spun in the dim light filtering through the solitary window that Gerald wandered toward.

My heart hammered as he bent down in front of a pockmarked and scratched dresser, pulling open the bottom drawer.

I didn't really know what to do, and so just stood there waiting for him to retrieve whatever it was he wanted to get.

Finally, after a few frustrating seconds of him selecting some papers from the messy piles inside the drawer, he stood and handed something each to Vicky and I.

"Here," he said. "Look through this. It's letter from the doctors, along with some of the notices about my father's pensions. It's all here. Feel free to look through the drawer, too. I want to cooperate as much as possible."

"Thank you," I said.

He stepped back, allowing us to move closer.

I knelt down, glancing briefly at the paper he'd handed me. It was dated three weeks prior, acknowledging another withdrawal for the pension at three hundred and seventy-two dollars.

No wonder he wanted these checks to keep coming. That wasn't a small amount of money.

"He was telling the truth about the cancer diagnosis," Vicky said. "It's all right here. I recognize the doctor's letterhead from when I had the kids."

It certainly looked like it was all there. Craig would be pleased. Not pleased with the amount of paperwork, but pleased at how quickly he'd be able to tie up the loose ends –

The sound of a door closing sent a shockwave down my spine.

Springing to my feet, I dashed to the stairs.

My heart began to thunder in my chest.

The door at the bottom had been shut...and Gerald was nowhere in sight.

"What's going on?" Vicky asked, looking wildly around. "Where is – "

I rushed down the stairs. "Gerald?" I called, my throat tight. How could I have been so stupid? Why didn't I listen to my gut feelings? Why did I follow him up here – "Gerald!"

"It's nothing personal, you know," came his dull voice, muffled by the door between us. "I just think I could squeeze a little bit more time out of this, is all."

All the danger bells began to ring inside my head. "Wait, Gerald – " I said. "What do you mean?"

"I had this all planned out, and then that stupid dog wandered into my backyard and ruined it. I had successfully kept everyone at arm's length for some time, and know I could have done it for a few months more. I had all sorts of stories ready to make up. And you all would have believed them, just like you did before."

"That's where you're wrong," I said. "I knew something wasn't right. So did the deputy. We were not going to let this all go until we figured out what happened to you and your dad."

"What are you going to do?" Vicky asked, hurrying down the stairs after me.

"I'm just going to go make sure Dad is buried again. Can't have another dog coming along to dig him up, can I?" he asked.

I laid my hand on the door handle and tried it; as I'd expected, it wouldn't give.

"Gerald, open this door," I said, knowing how futile the demand would be.

"Sorry, Miss Hollis, can't do that," he said. "See, I kind of figured something out when we were talking. If I find a way to cover all this up again, I might be able to squeeze a little bit more out of this like I planned."

"You'd be crazy to try," I said. "Once I tell my brother – "

"Oh, by the time your brother gets here, I'll be long gone," he said. "I've got a plan, don't worry."

"What is your plan, exactly?" I asked, the blood rushing in my ears. "Gerald? What are you planning?"

No answer on the other side of the door.

"Gerald? Gerald!"

I jostled the handle, but it wouldn't give.

I shoved my weight against it, but still it wouldn't budge.

I slammed my hand against the wood. Pain burst across my palm, like tiny shards of glass had sliced the skin.

"What happened?" Vicky asked. "What did he say?"

"He said he was going to cover it up again," I said. I glanced up at her, where she stood three stairs above me. "He locked us in here."

Her eyes widened. "Locked – are you kidding?"

"No," I said. "I wish I was."

"We need to get out of here!" she exclaimed.

"Okay, we need to try and stay calm," I said. "Otherwise we are going to be stuck here until he lets us out."

She nodded, but it was clearly reluctant. "Okay. Okay, what do we do?"

"We have to find another way out," I said.

She opened her mouth to argue, but then snapped it shut again. "How?"

"I don't know," I said. "We might be able to find a key or something and get out."

"Let's look, then," she said, and she climbed the stairs once more.

I swept my hand over the top of the doorframe, but wasn't terribly surprised to find it empty. There was no hook beside the door, no mat to hide anything underneath. I checked the edges of the steps, checked at the top of the stairs, looking along the banister. The slanted roof held nothing, at least not from what I could see.

I looked around, and Vicky stood at the window. "This is the only way out aside from the door," she said. She looked at me. "It's…a long way down."

It didn't look like there was even a lock to flip in the window. "I don't think it opens," I said. "So unless we break it – "

"We don't have to do that, do we?" she asked. "There's got to be another way out of here."

"You're right…" I said with a sigh, turning away.

I examined the room through a new lens; survival. It had become imperative that we leave the house, because now Gerald had changed the game on us. "What a liar…" I mumbled under my breath, walking toward the opposite wall. "I should have expected he'd do this – "

"Uh, Barbara?"

Vicky's question came out strained, and when I

turned to look at her, her mouth hung open as she gazed out the window. Her forefinger, pressed against the glass, trembled slightly.

"What's the matter?" I asked.

"Gerald's outside..." she said. "He's – he's getting something out of the shed."

"What?" I asked, going to kneel with her at the window.

I looked through the glass, bending my head to be able to see the shed on the other side of the yard. I could barely see it, but she was right; he had taken something from there, and had started back toward the house.

"That's not a gasoline can, is it?" she asked.

My heart skipped. "He wouldn't – no, why would he?" I asked. "That can't be – "

She rounded on me, eyes round and shining with fear. "Barbara, he's going to set fire to the house!"

"Why would he do that?" I asked. "That'd be insane. He wanted the house. He wanted to sell it. How could he if he burns it to the ground?"

"What if he has insurance?" she asked. "Or the bank – maybe the bank would help cover the cost of the house, especially if he claims it was an accident."

"Or something we started..." I breathed,

watching him walk closer and closer, taking slow, deliberate steps. He wouldn't want anyone thinking he was doing anything suspicious, would he? "How could we disprove him if we're – "

"We've got to get out of here!" Vicky wailed, shaking my shoulders. "I can't die here! What'll happen to my kids? My husband?"

"It's okay, we aren't going to die up here," I said, trying to infuse my words with some assurance, though I hardly felt any confidence myself. "Maybe we need to try kicking the door down. We won't have long once he starts the fire."

"And that could be any second," Vicky said. "He's looking around the edge of the house, now, probably trying to find the best place to start it."

Panic threatened to wash over me, my breathing coming in harsh snatches. I gripped my knees, digging the fingernails into my flesh, willing the pain to clear my head.

To remind me that I was *alive*. And unless we did something now, that might not be the case for very much longer.

Gritting my teeth, I stood up again and looked wildly around the room. Surely, there'd be something in this room that we could use to break the window.

Sure enough, I spotted a crowbar when I started to dig behind some of the broken chairs along the far wall. Coughing, I pulled it free from where it leaned against the wall, likely for years, and unearthed cobwebs and dust bunnies into the air.

"You know, I guess it makes sense that he's trying to do this," Vicky said in a hollow voice from across the room. "We know too much now. Might as well get rid of us. He can keep this thing going, like he said."

"Yes, well, now he's definitely going to end up in jail for attempted arson and murder," I said as I started back to her.

Vicky knelt at the window, staring down into the yard, horrified. "He's got a box of matches out now," she said, her voice eerily calm. She looked up at me. "At least, he did a few seconds ago. I have no idea where he is now..." Her gaze became distant. "Probably at the other side of the house, setting it ablaze."

"Stand back, Vicky," I said, but didn't give her much of an option when I pulled her up to her feet. She allowed me to drag her away, putting her out of harm's way.

I still had no idea how we were going to get down from a third story window, but that was a problem for after the window was broken.

I've got to make sure I break away enough of the glass so we don't slice our arms open on our way out –

I raised my hand to strike the glass, but a crashing noise at the bottom of the stairs forced me to turn around.

The maniac's come all the way up here to start the fire at the top! He wants to make sure that he gets us!

14

"Barb!"

I froze at the top of the stairs, the crowbar raised above my head. I'd very nearly let it fly, but the sight of my brother standing at the bottom stayed my hand.

It fell to the floor beside me with a loud *clang*. "Craig!" I exclaimed.

He and I met halfway on the stairs, and I threw myself into his arms.

"You're all right!" he said, looking me over. "I didn't know what to expect!"

"How did you find us?" I asked.

Vicky appeared at the top of the stairs.

"The boys called me, said that they saw you and Mrs. Foster go inside Mr. Thompson's house," he said. "They thought you'd been gone too long, and so they came outside to look for you. When they did, they saw you in the backyard and then following Gerald into the house."

I beamed at him. "Remind me to double their Christmas presents, will you?"

He laughed. "I'm just so glad you're all right."

"I'm fine," I said. "Now that you're here."

"Come on, let's get you both out of here."

He grabbed my hand and pulled me down the rest of the stairs.

I turned and looked over my shoulder; Vicky hurried along after me, her arms drawn in on herself as she looked wildly around.

"Where's Gerald?" I asked, Vicky's frantic searching quickening my own heart.

"Outside in the car," Craig said. "Roger will have handled him."

Roger! Of course he'd be here, too!

"What happened?" Vicky asked, hurrying to catch up to us at the top of the main staircase, headed down.

"Well..." Craig said, taking a visual sweep of the downstairs as soon as it came into sight. "I started to wonder about what Barb had been saying about this place. She'd been suspicious for some time about it, and when the boys told me that you two had disappeared inside here, all the alarms went off in my head."

We came to the front door, which stood open.

I paused, staring at it. *Craig didn't even take the time to close the door. He was so worried about us that he tore right up the stairs without wasting a precious second.*

I stared at the side of my brother's face as he shepherded us over the threshold, out into the darkening afternoon. Thunder rumbled in the distance, low and menacing in the east.

The police car was in the driveway, slightly askew, with Roger leaning on the hood. He looked up at our approach, unfolding his arms.

His eyes fell on me first, widening.

"You're all right," he said. I didn't think I'd ever heard that level of concern in his voice.

I nodded, my answer caught in my throat.

"Thank God..."

"What's the status?" Craig asked.

Roger glanced behind him as he rubbed his hand over the back of his neck. "Secured. Cuffed and locked in. Awaiting your decision about what to do with him."

"Get him down to the station," Craig said. "I can't stand the sight of him."

"Will do, boss," Roger said.

He spared me one last glance before circling the car and climbing into the driver's seat.

"Come on, I'll take you both back to our house," Craig said.

I let him lead me along, but I chanced another look at Roger as he pulled away.

He seemed genuinely worried about me. It was the same expression I'd seen on his face when we had been cornered in the Nelson's house. This time, though, we'd been separated.

It's almost as if I could see the regret on his face. The guilt that he wasn't there for me this time.

"I'm sorry that I didn't do something about this sooner..." Craig said. "You had every right to be concerned, it seems."

"How did you find Gerald?" I asked as we crossed from the Thompson's front yard into our own.

"Walking around the house upending a gas canister," Craig said. "It's not hard to discern what his plans were with that."

My stomach twisted. "My word, you got here just in the nick of time."

"Sure did," he said. "I asked him what he was up to, and he told me he was gardening."

I stared at Craig. I didn't know I could feel more shocked than I already did.

"What's going to happen to the house with all that gasoline around it?" Vicky asked.

"Nothing," Craig said. "The gasoline will dissipate, and the rain coming will wash the rest of it away."

I looked over my shoulder at the looming clouds. "I wonder if it would have saved us, if he had set the house on fire."

"Not unless it started beforehand..." Craig said. "But it doesn't matter. You're safe. And the house isn't in any danger of catching fire now."

He opened the front door, thunderous footsteps racing through the house greeting us on the other side. "Aunt Barbara! Aunt Barbara!"

I opened my arms just as the twins collided with me.

"We were so worried," Tim said into my shoulder.

I squeezed him more tightly. "I'm fine. It's okay. Your dad and Deputy Elwood protected us." I looked at him, smiling. "Just like they always do."

He smiled back.

"What happened? What happened?" Toby asked, hurrying to his dad who was helping Vicky down onto the couch; she still seemed a little lost in her thoughts, unsteady on her feet.

"Did you get him?" Tim asked.

Craig turned to glare at his son. "What do you mean, did I get him? What makes you think that anything – "

"We saw Roger cramming that guy into the back of the police car," Toby said, his thumb pointing over his shoulder.

Craig released a breath he'd been holding onto, shaking his head. "Yes…we got him." He then turned to me. "Have a seat, I'll get you both some sweet tea."

"That'd be great…" Vicky said, adjusting herself to be a bit more comfortable on the sofa.

"What are you going to do about old Mr. Thompson?" I asked. I didn't know how much Craig would want the boys to know, so I kept my question vague.

Craig peered back out into the living room, his brow furrowed. "I didn't see him there. Where was he?"

I stared at him. "Craig…you didn't see him?"

He shook his head, and started back for the door. "How in the world did I miss him?"

I shot a frantic look at Vicky, who looked equally as mortified.

I followed him out onto the front porch, and as soon as he closed the door, I hissed under my breath, "Craig, he's *dead*. In the backyard."

Craig paused, arm partially slid through the sleeve of his leather sheriff's jacket.

A growl of thunder crawled through the sky, the wind starting to pick up. "You didn't see the grave in the backyard?" I whispered.

"I was a little preoccupied..." he said, glancing toward the Thompson house. He sighed heavily. "This just got a lot more difficult."

"You really didn't know?" I asked.

"No, I thought we were just locking his son up for attempted arson and kidnapping..." he said. "And now we've got to slap murder onto that paperwork, too."

I shook my head. "He claims his father died of natural causes. I doubt you'll get him to admit anything else."

His brow furrowed. "What? Why in the world would he do that?"

"Bury him but not tell anyone?" I asked.

He nodded.

"He said he wanted to collect his father's pension

checks that were coming in. Said he planned to store up enough of them and *then* come clean so that he could turn around and use that money to buy a new house, and start over somewhere."

Craig sighed. His eyes drifted toward the front window, and when I followed his gaze, we spotted the twins sitting on the couch, leaning over the back to watch us.

They bolted when they were caught.

"You might have to start hiring them, purely because of the fact that they live with you and hear too much," I said.

"Yeah, well…I'd kind of hoped to keep the both of them away from my line of work. Maybe get them into law school, or convince them to be veterinarians or something else."

"You can't blame them if they'd want to follow after their daddy," I said.

Hands on his hips, he looked at me with a raised eyebrow. "I can and I will," he said. "Same reason I don't want *you* mixed up in this…yet you continue to do as you please."

"I swear, this time I was trying my best to keep my distance – "

Craig turned and walked back into the house; rain had begun to pelt the driveway in fat, quarter-sized drops. There'd be nothing he could do to exhume Mr. Thompson until the rain stopped.

"Roger told me that you two were in cahoots on our way over here," Craig said to me, even as he let me step past him to get out of the blowing rain first. "Don't lie to me."

My heart sank, and I frowned as he closed the door behind us. "Well, *this* time, I wasn't going over there to snoop. Vicky and I both heard a dog barking, and Mrs. Benson had come by yesterday asking if we'd seen their dog – " Then I gasped. "Oh, I forgot about Dixie!"

"Don't worry," Craig said, crossing his arms. "I had Roger take her home as soon as he locked Gerald up in the backseat."

"Oh, good..." Vicky said, laying a hand on her heart. "I was just in here thinking the same thing. Poor thing, we left her on that couch downstairs – she probably thought she was going to get more of those treats."

"I'm just glad she's okay, too," I said.

"Safe and sound, as far as I know," Craig said. "Roger would've said otherwise."

Then I smirked at Craig.

"Roger really trusted that backseat to hold

Gerald while he took Dixie home?" I asked. "That seems a little foolish."

"Trust me, he wasn't going anywhere, even if he tried."

"Not that he probably would have tried in the first place," Vicky said with a shiver. "He didn't seem to have any life in him, did he? Didn't care about anything."

"Cared enough about his own possible future to set the house on fire with us in it," I said.

She and I looked at each other...and I didn't know if it was the fact we were sitting on the couch in Craig's living room and the danger had long since passed, but we both laughed. I laughed so hard that my belly ached and tears streamed down my face.

"Aunt Barbara's lost her mind..." Toby said. "It's official."

Collecting myself, not spared of some hiccups, I picked up one of the throw pillows on the couch and tossed it at the boy.

"Oh, my..." Vicky said, wiping both her forefingers beneath her eyes in a sweep, clearing any smudged mascara. "I really shouldn't stay. I appreciate the offer for the sweet tea, Sheriff, but I should be getting home. My family will be back soon."

"I'd really rather you waited here," Craig said.

"I'll be happy to go over with you and explain everything that happened to your husband."

This satisfied Vicky, and she resumed her seat beside me.

Craig sat down in his armchair. "Might as well sit down, boys. Seems you have little interest in listening to me about these things."

Toby obediently sat down at his father's feet, but Tim heaved a sigh behind him.

"Hey, wait – "

But Tim had already grabbed his brother by the scruff of his shirt and started hauling him off out of the room. "It's really not our business, Toby."

"But Dad said we could!"

The two squabbled as they made their way out of sight.

"Well...is there anything else you two need to tell me?" Craig asked. "Anything that Gerald said or did that would be good for me to know?"

I glanced at Vicky.

She shrugged. "I suppose just that he seemed so...dead himself. He had no emotion. Didn't care that his father had died. Didn't care that he was going to set the house on fire with us inside... It is just rather odd, isn't it?"

"It is indeed," Craig said. "Which leaves me to

wonder, will he actually tell me the truth about what happened with his father? If he doesn't care about anyone or anything..."

"I think he will," I said. "I think, deep down, that he did care. When he saw the pie Vicky had brought for him and his dad, I could see a glimmer of what I now know was grief. It might have been brief, but it was there."

Craig nodded. "Well, I suppose there's a lot that went on in that house that we'll never fully know the answer to," he said.

Thunder clapped and the rain began in earnest outside. All three of us fell silent then, and turned to watch the storm out the window.

15

"I appreciate your patience, young lady," said the kind man with deep set wrinkles around his eyes. He smiled at me from beneath his thick, grey moustache, the only hair on his whole head apart from wispy eyebrows. "This shouldn't take too much longer."

I smiled at the man, loosening the scarf I'd wound so close around my throat before stepping foot out of the house. The rain had not let up yet, and might have even settled in for a long, hard pour over the town for the rest of the day.

My eventful morning might have set me back, but that doesn't mean I still don't have the last few things I need to do before Christmas Eve comes tomorrow!

Craig thought I'd been crazy for wanting to leave

at all after the day I'd had, but I insisted that I had to make it here, to the bank, before they closed at five. I glanced up at the large, gold-numbered clock on the wall.

Besides...I couldn't possibly stay there at the house all by myself, stewing on everything. This is better for my sanity, to be out doing something.

"I'm sorry I'm here so close to the end of the day, but I had...well, some things held me up today," I said.

The man continued to smile, looking up at me from the paperwork he'd been filling out for me. "Oh, it's quite all right, my dear. No trouble at all. Ol' Smithy is here to help, you mark my words. I'm just happy I could help."

He hadn't blinked an eye when I'd walked in here a quarter of an hour before and informed him that I wanted to open a savings account. In fact, he got right to work getting everything in order for me.

It had been easier than I thought, too. I'd dragged my feet about doing this for weeks, even though I knew that I had every intention of staying in town for at least the foreseeable future.

This is the best way I can show Craig that I don't need to rely on him like a child, but also that I mean to stay. And this way, I can tuck away some of the last of the money I brought with me from Liberty City.

It felt good, too, making this sort of decision. I knew I needed to set more permanent roots down. It was time.

"Here we are," Mr. Smithy said, passing me a sheet of paper. "Does everything look right?"

The twins had no idea why it mattered, told me it was silly to go to the bank right before Christmas. They thought maybe I'd saved all my shopping for the last minute. Craig, however, gave me his blessing to go. If it wasn't something as concrete as this, he probably would have insisted I stay home after the fiasco that happened at the Thompson household.

"Yes, everything's correct," I said with a grin, handing it back.

"Very well, and with the funds you have chosen to start the account with..." He reached beneath the counter, procuring a checkbook as well as a golden key. He handed them to me. "Now, is there anything else I can help you with today?"

"No, sir, you have been most helpful," I said. "Thank you. This means a great deal."

He chuckled. "Oh, it's not all that great," he said. "It's just a bank account."

"Have a merry Christmas," I said.

"And you as well, Miss. You as well."

I headed back out to brave the wet, chilly afternoon. The rain had slowed to an irritating drizzle that clung to my skin, my eyelashes nearly freezing as I squinted my eyes shut against the wind that whipped down the sidewalk.

"I thought I recognized that truck."

I nearly tripped over my boots, swinging my umbrella around…and found myself standing face to face with Ricky Booker.

"Ricky…" I breathed, staring at him, then staring past him down a narrow alleyway between the bank and the business beside it. For a moment, I thought he had appeared out of thin air.

"Hello, Barbara," he said, that charming smile of his curling up the side of his face. "It's good to see you. I'd hoped I would get a chance to see your pretty face again."

Grateful that the chill in the air had already drawn a flush to my face, I smiled warily. It had been a few weeks since I'd seen him. More than that, wasn't it? Maybe even closer to two months. All I could do was laugh nervously.

"I heard things didn't work out with our old friend Stewart Wilson," he said, sliding his hands into the pockets of his trousers. "Sorry to hear that."

"No, it was for the best," I said. "He...well, he turned out to be – "

"Not such a nice guy, eh?" he asked, that smile of his still firmly in place. "I tried to tell you that night. I definitely tried to tell you, but you were so mad at me that you just couldn't see it."

I didn't argue with him. *Why is he waiting here to talk to me?*

With a terrifying jolt, I had the horrible thought that he might try to attack me, right then and there.

I stared at that smile of his, trying to see if it was nothing but hatred behind his handsome eyes, or forgiveness.

Honestly, it was hard to tell either way.

"You're right..." I said with another nervous laugh, shrugging. "I should have listened to you."

"I only ever had your best interests at heart," he said. "Though...it might not have been the other way around."

I stiffened, and not from the cold.

I knew that word of my involvement in the downfall of his illegal gambling operation would have gotten back to him. With Craig looking into it, there really could only have been one person he would have heard it from.

He would have to suspect me. I'm the sheriff's sister.

Ricky shook his head. "Look…I don't want you to think that you have to avoid me forever, okay? I thought it best to break the ice between us. I didn't want you thinking I had any hard feelings."

"Hard feelings?" I asked, more feebly than I should have. *This is just not my day today –*

"I knew that my underground ring would be broken up sooner or later," he said smoothly, turning his face up to the spattering rain, letting it glance off his cheeks. He squinted up toward the heavens. "In all honesty, it was too difficult dealing with that as well as trying to run the restaurant. Too many different plates in the air, so to speak."

"I can imagine it was…" I said.

"I just wanted you to know that I bear you no ill will," he said. "And I'd like for you to feel free to come down to the restaurant anytime you'd like. I'd be happy to serve you some of my latest creations."

"I appreciate the offer, I really do," I said. "That's very kind of you."

He smirked, looking back over at me. "I know that you turned me down, but for some reason…I just can't seem to let you go. You're too interesting, Miss Barbara Hollis. Maybe it's because of the family you come from. Or the fact that you're from the big city. Like a duck out of water."

I really couldn't let this get to me. His attraction might have been endearing at one point, but now...I just couldn't quite tell if it frightened me or enticed me.

"Well, it is good to see you, Ricky," I said. "But with Christmas Eve being tomorrow, I have so much that I still have to do, and Craig's back at the house waiting for me – "

"No, no, of course, go ahead," he said, taking a step back, sweeping his arm out. "By all means. I hope you and your family have a wonderful Christmas. And if you're feeling at all peckish during that lazy week between Christmas and New Year's, why don't you keep my little establishment in mind?"

I laughed. "Sure, I'll make sure to say something to Craig," I said.

I'm sure Craig would love that idea.

He turned and started up the sidewalk, giving me a wave. "Have a wonderful Christmas, Barbara. I'll see you around."

"Yes, I'll see you."

I didn't dare glance in the rearview mirror until I'd pulled away from the sidewalk, leaving the bank some distance behind.

I really should probably avoid him. I don't want to

test him to find out if his magnanimous attitude is genuine or not.

I breathed a sigh of relief, and started for home.

All that behind me, all I have to do is focus on Christmas. The Thompson situation is resolved, and then whatever that was with Ricky is behind me...

None of those things mattered now.

All that mattered was that I would be spending the next few days with Craig and the boys. I'd gotten my wish this year.

This was going to be the best Christmas ever.

16

The soothing tune of a familiar Christmas carol played on the radio.

"Open mine next, open mine!" Toby hollered, clambering over his brother to grab a rather messily wrapped gift tucked underneath the back of the tree. With extensive effort, he shoved it into his father's lap where he sat in his favorite armchair.

Craig looked over at me, smirking. "Well, thanks Toby," he said.

Peeling back the tape, his eyes lit up, and I wasn't all that surprised to see that it was genuine. "Wow, Toby!" he exclaimed, lifting out a black, leather strap with a single button fastened to the side. "What is it?"

Toby plopped himself down beside his father on the floor like an expectant puppy. "I made it myself! It's a holster for your flashlight, so you can hang it right from your bedpost!"

Craig threw back his head and laughed. "I have been saying how I hate trying to find it in the middle of the night, haven't I?" he asked.

"You sure have," Toby said, beaming. "I made it in shop class."

Craig reached out and laid a hand on his son's shoulder. "Thank you, son," he said. "It's a wonderful gift. I can't wait to use it."

I smiled as Toby's face exploded with delight.

This is all he wanted. What all three of them wanted. Just to be together today.

Truth be told…it was all I had wanted today, too.

"Aunt Barb, why don't you open one next?" Tim asked, swinging around with a present already selected in hand. "It's from Dad."

I glanced at Craig, and he nodded. "Go on," he said, smiling. "You'll like that, I think."

I accepted the gift from Tim, admiring the care that Craig had taken to wrap it. "It's beautiful paper," I said. "I love the poinsettias."

"Open it!" Toby said.

I slit open the paper and unfolded it, revealing a slim, black velvet box.

I looked up at him, surprised.

His smile widened.

I opened the box and found a slender, golden chain with a single charm hanging from it, a golden heart with a solitary sapphire shimmering in the center.

"I know it's not as flashy as some of the jewelry you have," he said. "And I know that you always wear that necklace Gram gave you – "

"Craig, it's beautiful!" I said. "I absolutely love it."

It was the truth. As simple and small as it was, it was such a personal thing to know that he paid such close attention to me that he recognized how I enjoyed wearing jewelry.

"The boys and I all went and picked it out together," he said. "We wanted you to know that we love you and are so happy that you've come to stay with us."

My eyes stung as I looked up at him, and then each of the twins in turn. "I...I don't know what to say."

"You don't have to say anything, really," Tim said with a shrug.

"Yeah, thanks would be fine," Toby said.

His brother tossed a wad of wrapping paper at him.

"Thank you…" I said. At once, I reached up and unhooked the clasp of Gram's necklace. It was the first time I'd taken it off since I'd gotten it fixed. Part of me had worn it so intentionally as a means of honoring Frankie, the jeweler who had been the one to repair it before he was murdered, but that time was over. It could return to my jewelry box and remain there as a treasure.

I slipped on the new necklace, and the clasp fastened easily. I smiled as it settled over the top of my sweater, sparkling brightly against the red beneath it. "It's wonderful. I love it more than you know."

"Good," Craig said.

"And now, it's your turn," I said, getting up from the couch and going to fetch my gifts for him. I stacked three, four, five gifts on top of one another, and then handed them all over to him.

Peering around the stack of gifts at me, he frowned. "What is all this?"

"Just go ahead and open them," I said, pulling my legs up underneath me and settling back against the couch cushions. I smiled, playing with the little sapphire charm around my neck, admiring the way it caught the amber glow from the fireplace.

Craig set a few of the gifts on the floor beside him, and opened the one from the bottom.

His face went slack, mouth falling open. He turned to look up at me, shock paling his face.

"What is it, Dad?" Toby asked. "What'd she get you?"

The twins climbed over their own gifts to look over the arms of his chair.

Toby furrowed his brow, looking up at me. "I don't get it."

"Is it...a toy?" Tim asked.

"Not just a *toy*," Craig said, pulling the box free from the wrapping. He turned it over. "It's Captain Michaels! Barb, how in the world did you find one?"

I grinned. "I have my ways."

He beamed at the boys. "This was a toy I wanted when I was your age, boys. I never got one, though."

"Never got one?" Toby asked.

Tim looked at me. "So you got it for him now?"

Craig laughed in disbelief as he opened the next gift. "A real pair of Explorer's Binoculars?" and then the next, "An Atlantis comic? First edition?"

The boys seemed confused about their Dad getting so excited over some toys.

"Barb…" he said, looking at the gifts I'd gotten him. "I have no idea how you found some of these, but it means a great deal to me."

I smiled. "I'm glad you like them."

He showed the boys the toys, and just as they were unwrapping the binoculars, a knock sounded at the door.

"I'll get it," I said, hopping to my feet.

I padded over to the door, opened it up and –

"Deputy Elwood," I said, smiling. "Right on time."

"Roger, hey! Come on in!" Craig said from his chair.

I stepped aside, and Roger came in, carrying several gifts himself.

"Looks like your Christmas is off to a great start," he said, eyeing the stack of toys near the tree.

The twins hurried back over to show him all the things we'd gotten for them, talking over one another.

An hour or so passed, after Roger had given the boys their gifts and Craig his – a new Sheriff's hat, since his was getting a little tattered. Craig and the boys had gone into the kitchen to finish up the eggnog and serve it to us before dinner.

"And there's something here for you, too," Roger

said, reaching beside him on the other side of the couch, out of my sight. He procured yet another present, and passed it to me.

"For me?" I asked. "But I didn't get you anything."

He shrugged. "That's not the point, is it?"

"No, I guess it's not," I said, hesitantly taking the gift.

My cheeks started to burn as I set it on my lap, feeling his gaze on the side of my face. I had no idea what to expect. What could it be? Why had he gone out of his way to get me something like this?

My heart skipped when I pulled back the paper and opened the plain, white box.

"A...Sally Anne doll..." I breathed.

I looked over at him, the color in my face only deepening.

"What...?" I asked, looking at him. "How did you –"

"Got the idea when we were talking about Craig's gift," he said. "You mentioned you never had one. I spotted one when I was out one afternoon. Thought you might like it."

I brushed the doll's blonde hair out of her blue, glass eyes. Her rosy cheeks looked almost real, and her red dress had been embroidered with little white roses.

"She's even more beautiful than I remembered," I said, looking up at him. "I…don't know what to say."

He smiled at me, a small, warm smile. "You are quite welcome," he said. "I had hoped you would like it."

For a man who made an effort to tell me that he didn't approve of my involvement in the work he and my brother were doing, a man who had ridiculed me, belittled me, and teased me…I wondered if I had read him wrong.

I wondered if we had gotten off on the wrong foot.

"Wait here," I said, getting to my feet.

I hurried past the boys in the kitchen, who were trying to decide how much nutmeg they wanted to add to the eggnog, and only had to look around for a moment before I found what I was looking for.

I returned to the living room, and my heart skipped when I looked at Roger.

I'd never really thought him handsome. Compared to some of the men in my past, he would be rather plain.

He did, however, have a great deal more character than any of the men I'd known. And a big heart, something I could have only seen by interacting with him like I had over the last few months. He never seemed to have a desire to hide who he really was, and as such, I truly believed that I had a chance to see the real Roger.

I sat down beside him on the couch, and handed him a small book.

"What's this?" he asked, turning it over.

"One of my favorites," I said. "Something I read a lot when I lived in Liberty City. Kept me company."

He looked at me, and smiled. "Been a while since I read a good book. Thank you. I look forward to reading it, knowing it meant so much to you."

My cheeks flushed again, and I smiled. "Well, good. I don't need it back, either. It's yours."

"Thank you," he said.

We sat in quiet for a moment, and I gazed down at the doll with disbelief.

To think he had listened so closely to such an offhand comment...

"Here's some eggnog!" called Toby, hurrying into the living room, the pair of mugs in his hands sloshing as he brought them over to us on the couch.

I took one with a laugh, and handed it to Roger.

Toby chortled and raced back into the kitchen.

"Hey, Barb, how long does this ham need?" Craig called out to me.

"It's done, I'm just keeping it warm," I said. "We can eat whenever you want."

Everyone in the kitchen cheered.

Roger smiled at me, raising his mug. "Merry Christmas," he said, holding it out to me.

"Merry Christmas," I said, and we clinked our mugs together.

CONTINUE the mysterious adventures of Barbara Hollis with "The Happy Housekeeper's Guide to Crime: A Barbara Hollis Murder Mystery, Book 6."

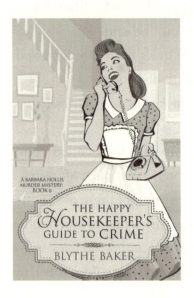

ABOUT THE AUTHOR

Blythe Baker is the lead writer behind several popular historical and paranormal mystery series. When Blythe isn't buried under clues, suspects, and motives, she's acting as chauffeur to her children and head groomer to her household of beloved pets. She enjoys walking her dogs, lounging in her backyard hammock, and fiddling with graphic design. She also likes binge-watching mystery shows on TV. To learn more about Blythe, visit her website and sign up for her newsletter at www.blythebaker.com

Made in United States
Troutdale, OR
04/17/2024

19265339R00159